THE **HARDY BOYS**®

#178

THE MYSTERY OF THE BLACK RHINO

FRANKLIN W. DIXON

Aladdin Paperbacks
New York London Toronto Sydney Singapore

First Aladdin Paperbacks edition April 2003

Copyright © 2003 by Simon & Schuster, Inc.

ALADDIN PAPERBACKS
An imprint of Simon & Schuster
Children's Publishing Division
1230 Avenue of the Americas
New York, NY 10020

The text of this book was set in New Caledonia.

Printed in the United States of America
2 4 6 8 10 9 7 5 3 1

Library of Congress Control Number 2002107370

ISBN 0-689-85598-2

Whispers of Murder

"Anybody here?" Joe called.

When nobody answered, they decided to make their way toward the interior of the shop, thinking that perhaps someone might be in a stockroom. They passed shelves of ornate African masks, baskets, and carvings of all kinds of animals that people normally associate with Africa

"Where are the mounted big-game heads?" Joe asked.

"You've seen too many old movies," Frank said. "With so many species nearly extinct, people go on photo safaris today. They don't go to kill the animals."

Joe was just about to call out again when they heard a door open.

"If you want it killed, then I'm your man," a voice said. "Don't ever forget that."

The Hardy Boys Mystery Stories

Available from ALADDIN Paperbacks

Contents

THE MYSTERY OF THE
BLACK RHINO

1 The Threat on the Subway

"Frank and Joe Hardy in Africa!" Chet Morton turned around and grinned at seventeen-year-old Joe Hardy, who was sitting in the backseat of Chet's borrowed convertible. "Sounds like the name of a really bad movie."

"Yeah—just keep your eyes on the road, Morton!" Joe said with a grin. "Too bad you'll be sitting in class, listening to Mr. Bannerman talk about Africa, while Frank and I will actually *be* there."

"You guys are so lucky," Chet complained. "I wish my dad were a famous detective so he could get invited to places like Kenya."

"It would be fun if we could all go," Joe said. "Just think of all the stuff we'd do."

"I know," Chet said.

1

"Hey, Chet, could you just drop us off in front of Fifth Avenue Africana, circle the block, and then pick us up?" eighteen-year-old Frank Hardy asked. "It would certainly make our lives a lot easier."

Chet shook his head. "I've got this all worked out, Frank. I'm taking you guys to the Pelham Bay Park subway station. It's just a couple of blocks from my aunt's apartment in the Bronx. The Number Six train will take you down Lexington Avenue. Then you can cross over to Fifth Avenue and take care of your business."

"I thought you liked to drive in Manhattan," Frank said.

"I do, but Mom said I needed to help my aunt pack. She's getting kind of forgetful, and Mom wants to make sure she has everything she needs to spend a few weeks with us," Chet said. "I'll meet you in front of the subway station in three hours. I have to be back in Bayport by seven tonight so I can go to work."

"Okay," Frank said. He looked back at Joe. "If you hadn't forgotten to check the battery in the van like I told you to, we wouldn't . . ." He stopped. He and Joe had been over this before, so there was no use in having another argument.

Joe let it pass. He would have taken care of everything if the track coach hadn't given the team two more hours in the weight room because he thought they hadn't pushed themselves enough in the last couple of races.

"Why do you need to go into New York for books on Africa anyway?" Chet asked. "Don't they have books on Africa in the Bayport Library?"

"Not the ones Dad needs. These are about police procedures in East Africa," Frank said. "They're really hard to get, too. The owner of Fifth Avenue Africana agreed to lend them to Dad, though, and he can even take them to Kenya."

"He said—and here I quote—," added Joe, "'I'd be honored to let the great Fenton Hardy use books from my collection.'"

Chet smiled. "Here we are, guys. I'll be circling the block here in three hours, so be looking for me."

The Hardy boys nodded.

Chet pulled quickly into a no-parking zone, let Frank and Joe out, then rejoined traffic on the avenue.

Frank and Joe got their subway tokens at a booth near the turnstile, then headed to the platform for the train that would take them downtown.

"Good—it's not crowded!" Joe said when they reached the platform. "I don't like being jammed in a train like a sardine."

"It's not rush hour. We may have some trouble coming back up, though," Frank said. He nudged Joe and nodded toward a couple of teenage boys leaning against one of the girders. "Look how those guys are eyeing that woman's purse."

An elderly woman with a rather large black purse

was standing at the edge of the platform, unaware that she was being watched.

Just as the Hardy boys heard the train approaching, Frank said, "They know we're watching them. Maybe that'll keep them from trying anything."

"Yeah. And maybe they won't get on the train, either," Joe said. "They *do* look like trouble."

The train screeched to a halt, and the doors hissed open.

The Hardy boys waited just a minute to make sure the elderly woman got on the train safely, then they got on and sat a couple of seats away from her.

Just as the doors to the car started to close, the two teenage boys jumped aboard, too.

"Punks!" Frank whispered to Joe. "They're probably mad at us for keeping them from stealing her purse in the station."

"Yeah," Joe agreed.

He knew they had to be vigilant without antagonizing the two teens. The last thing they needed was to get involved in something that would keep them from meeting Chet and his aunt at the agreed time.

Frank pulled a subway map from his pocket and looked at it for several minutes. "We'll get off at Fifty-first Street," he said. "That way, we'll just be a couple of blocks or so from the bookstore."

Nothing happened between the boys and the older woman after the train had picked up and discharged passengers at several stations in the Bronx, so the Hardy boys began to relax.

They had begun to think that the two teens had forgotten about the elderly woman and her purse. Just as the train crossed the Harlem River into Manhattan and started slowing down for the 125th Street Station, though, the two suspicious-looking guys stood up and got ready to get off. They held on to the hand straps and started whispering to each other.

"They're going to try something," Joe whispered to Frank. "Get ready."

Now the train was coming into the station. Frank could see that the platform was crowded.

Just as the train stopped and the doors hissed open, the two punks made their move.

Joe had never seen such quickness.

One teen snatched the woman's purse and handed it to his friend, who was off and into the crowd in less than a blink of the eye. The original thief was right behind his friend.

The woman started screaming.

"We'll get your purse back for you!" Frank shouted.

Joe and Frank broke through the crowds of waiting passengers.

"Stop those kids! Stop them!" Joe shouted to anyone who might listen. "They stole a woman's purse!" His shouts seemed to be drowned out by a train arriving from downtown.

The doors of their train closed behind them, and the train sped on downtown.

"There they are!" Frank shouted.

Joe looked. The two boys were racing up the steps toward the street.

The Hardy boys ran after them.

When they reached the top of the steps, Frank and Joe could see the two teens heading east on 125th Street.

Frank knew they were in the part of New York City known as Spanish Harlem. His class had gone on a field trip to El Museo del Barrio last year. His art teacher had wanted the class to see the hundreds of *santos,* hand-carved wooden saints in the Spanish Catholic tradition.

The Hardy boys started after the two thieves.

"I bet those guys didn't expect we'd do this," Frank said. "They probably thought we wouldn't leave the platform. Let's keep them in sight until we can find a police officer."

"Yeah," Joe agreed.

The Hardy boys had to dodge traffic and pedestrians as they crossed against the light at Park Avenue.

Up ahead the two teens turned left at Madison Avenue. They were heading downtown.

"Where do you think they're going?" Frank asked. "We can't chase them all over Manhattan."

Joe shrugged.

Frank didn't have to wait long for an answer. As the two teens crossed 124th Street, they entered Marcus Garvey Park and headed down a secluded footpath.

"They're probably going to find a place to dump the purse once they've removed what they want," Joe said.

"Come on—let's pick up the pace!" Frank shouted.

With a burst of speed that would have pleased their track coach, the Hardy boys raced into Marcus Garvey Park.

Suddenly one of the punks looked behind him. Joe thought the expression on the guy's face was priceless.

"They can't believe it's us!" Frank shouted. "Come on. We'll show them why we won the state championship last month!"

The Hardy boys had almost reached the two teens when they suddenly veered off the path and into the woods.

When Frank and Joe reached the place where they thought the thieves had left the path, they stopped. "It's a little spooky here, even in the daytime," Frank said. "They could be hiding anywhere."

Just then the two punks rushed out of the trees toward them, catching the Hardy boys by surprise.

"Here's what you're looking for, man!" one of the teens said. He shoved the purse at Frank and took off. The force caused Frank to stumble against Joe.

They both tumbled to the ground in a heap.

"Hey! What was that all . . . ," Joe started to say. He looked up to find himself flanked by two police officers.

When Frank started to stand up, one officer drew his gun and said, "Stay where you are!"

"You don't understand, Officer," Frank protested. "We're not the ones who stole this purse."

"We know all about the fencing operation that operates out of this park, boys," the second officer said. "Why do you think we're here? We've been keeping this place under surveillance for several weeks."

"Our backup caught your two friends," the first officer said.

"They're not our friends," Frank said. "We were chasing them, trying to get the purse back for the woman on the subway."

"Yeah, yeah," the second officer said. "Keep talking. Maybe one of these years you'll make sense."

"We're not part of any fencing operation," Joe explained. "We're the ones who chased the guys who stole the purse."

"Leave the purse on the ground and stand up," the first officer said. "You can finish your story at the station."

"Great." Joe rolled his eyes. "We'll never get Dad's books now."

"That's what you get for doing a good deed,"

Frank said. Suddenly he had an idea. "Could I show you my driver's license?"

The second officer gave him a funny look. "What are you trying to pull? Most crooks don't want to be identified."

"I told you, Officer, we're not crooks," Frank explained. "I think if you'll take a look at my driver's license, this misunderstanding will all be cleared up."

"Take your wallet out slowly," the first officer said.

Frank began to remove his wallet. When it was out of his pocket, he handed it to the officer.

"Frank Hardy," the first officer read. "Bayport." He blinked and looked at Frank. "Are you? . . ."

Frank nodded. "We're Fenton Hardy's sons," he said. "Have you heard of him?"

"Have I heard of him? Have I heard of peanut butter and jelly? I'm Al Fielding," the first officer said. "My dad used to talk about Mr. Hardy all the time." He introduced the Hardy boys to the other officer, whose name was Randy. "Our dads were in the same precinct here in New York for several years, before yours decided to become a private detective."

"Why don't you let us tell you how all this happened?" Joe said. "You know we wouldn't steal a woman's purse."

"No way. Not Fenton Hardy's boys," Al said. "But I'll still need for you to fill out a report about what happened. Whoever handed you this purse is part of a gang that steals purses on the Number Six subway and then fences them here in Marcus Garvey Park."

"We know the drill," Frank said.

As they followed Al and Randy to their squad car, Frank explained where they had been headed when the purse snatching took place.

"We'll make this easy. We'll take you there, and on the way, Randy here can fill you in on this fencing operation," Al said. "It's the least we can do for your help with breaking up this ring."

As they headed to Fifth Avenue Africana in the patrol car, the Hardy boys gave the officers the full story.

"We had no idea we'd be breaking up a purse snatching ring," Joe said. "We just weren't going to let them get away with taking that woman's purse."

"Well, my dad always said that Fenton Hardy had the golden touch when it came to detective work," Al said. "It seems he's passed it down to his sons."

For the rest of the drive, the Hardy boys explained why they were going to Fifth Avenue Africana.

"Dad's been invited to speak at a conference of East African police organizations in Nairobi, Kenya," Frank said. "We're going with him. We've never been to Africa before."

"That'll be some trip," Al said as he pulled up to a store. "This should be it."

The front of the building had an ornately lettered

sign that read FIFTH AVENUE AFRICANA.

"Thanks for the ride!" Frank said. "Now we may be able to get Dad's books and meet Chet on time."

"Do you know how to get back to Pelham Bay Park?" Al asked.

Joe nodded. "We take the uptown Number Six at the Fifty-first Street Station," he said.

"Right," Al said.

The Hardy boys jumped out and thanked Al and Randy again for the ride downtown.

"Tell your dad that Big Al Fielding's son said hello," Al said.

"We'll do that," Joe said.

"If I have any more questions about the purse snatching," Al said, "I'll call you in Bayport before you leave for Africa." The police car pulled away from the curb and headed uptown.

Frank checked his watch. "We're in pretty good shape time-wise, Joe, but we need to hurry. Come on."

The shop door made a loud buzzing noise when they entered, but the darkened interior didn't reveal any clerks or customers.

"Maybe there just aren't a lot of people in New York City who are interested in Africana today," Frank observed.

"Maybe," Joe said. "Anybody here?" he called.

When nobody answered, they decided to make their way toward the interior of the shop, thinking

11

that perhaps someone might be in a stockroom. They passed shelves of ornate wooden and metal African masks, intricately woven baskets, and carvings of all kinds of animals that people normally associate with Africa—especially elephants, lions, rhinoceroses, and giraffes.

"Where are the mounted big-game heads?" Joe asked.

"You've seen too many old movies," Frank said. "With so many species nearly extinct, people go on photo safaris today. They don't go to kill the animals."

Joe was just about to call out again when they heard a door open.

"If you want it killed, then I'm your man," a voice said. "Don't ever forget that."

2 The Suspicious Passenger

The voice belonged to one of the biggest men the Hardy boys had ever seen. He was dressed in a safari jacket and a hunter's hat.

As the departing man pushed past them, Frank could see that his skin was sunburned. *He looks like he's just come back from a safari himself,* Frank thought.

"Wow," Joe whispered. "He looks pretty nasty!"

"You're telling me," Frank agreed. "He wouldn't have to shoot big game. One look at his face and the animals would be scared to death."

"May I help you?"

The boys turned toward the voice coming from the rear of the shop. In the dim light they could barely make out the form of another man. He was smaller than the first one, and dressed in casual clothes.

"We're Frank and Joe Hardy," Frank said. "We've come to pick up some books for our father, Fenton Hardy."

Immediately the man's total demeanor changed. He almost rushed toward them with a smile on his face and his hand extended.

"Oh, yes! This is indeed a pleasure! I'm Donald Watson, the owner of Fifth Avenue Africana," Watson said, as he grasped both of the Hardy boys' hands at once. "I wish your father could have come with you. I've always wanted to meet the famous Fenton Hardy."

"Dad's got so much work to do—to get ready for the conference—that he couldn't," Joe explained. "But he did send his best wishes and thanks for letting him borrow your books."

"Oh, it's my pleasure," Watson said. "They're in my office. Come. I'll get them for you. Would you care for something to drink? I think I have some soda in the fridge."

Frank glanced at his watch. Even after the detour to catch the purse snatchers, they were a little ahead of schedule. "Actually, I am kind of thirsty," he said. "What about you, Joe?"

"Me, too," Joe said. " A little super fast running in Manhattan will do that to you."

14

Watson gave them a puzzled look. As he removed two cans from his refrigerator, he asked, "Were you just jogging in the park?"

"Actually, we were running after some purse snatchers," Joe said. "Up in Spanish Harlem."

Frank explained what had happened. "For a while there, we weren't sure if we'd make it down here or not."

Joe thought he saw a look of apprehension on Watson's face, but it disappeared almost as quickly has it had appeared.

"Well, what could I expect from the sons of such a famous detective as Fenton Hardy?" Watson said. He smiled at them. "Of course, I'm sure you must hear that a lot."

Watson turned and started taking books off the shelf. "I've pulled all of the books from my collection that I think your father can use. I believe the two of you can manage them. I'll put them in some cloth shopping bags."

"Who was that man leaving the shop when we got here?" Joe asked.

Watson's hand hesitated just a minute before pulling the final book off the shelf. "His name is, uh, Jackson. He's a very unpleasant man who I wish would stay away from my shop," he replied. He turned and gave the Hardy boys a big smile. "What did you actually hear him say?" he asked.

"He was talking about *killing* something for you," Frank said. "He looked pretty serious."

"Well, *he* may be, but *I'm* not," Watson said. "Did you see any mounted heads or animal skins when you came into my shop?"

The Hardy boys shook their heads.

"There's a good reason for that. I don't deal in such things," Watson continued. "I won't be a part of the destruction of the world's wild animals."

The Hardy boys had read all about how many of the wild animals in Africa were in danger of extinction because of unscrupulous hunters and poachers.

"That's one of the things Dad will be talking about," Joe said. "He has some ideas that he thinks will help the police forces in East Africa deal with illegal hunters."

"We need more people like your father, then," Watson said. "The situation is getting worse, especially in certain countries."

Frank glanced at his watch again.

"Well, we'd better be going or we'll miss our ride back to Bayport," he said. He set his empty soft drink can down on a counter. "Thanks again for lending Dad the books, Mr. Watson. He'll probably deliver them to you in person when we get back from Kenya."

"I'll certainly look forward to the meeting," Watson said. He shook hands with both of the boys again. "Have a safe trip."

"Thanks," Joe said.

As the Hardy boys headed out of Fifth Avenue Africana, Joe took another look around. Even without big-game heads mounted on the wall or stacks of the skins of lions and leopards, there was something about the shop that filled him with excitement. He didn't know if it was because of all the old movies he had seen on television, but he knew the upcoming trip was going to be a wonderful experience.

Fifth Avenue was more crowded now than it had been when the boys went into the shop.

"People are starting to head home," Frank said, "but I think we can miss the big rush. Come on."

They hurried up to Fifty-first Street, then sped across Madison Avenue and Park Avenue. Finally they reached Lexington Avenue and the subway station that would take them back up to Pelham Bay Park.

They got their tokens and rushed to the uptown platform, getting there just as the Six train pulled in. The train was more crowded this time, so the Hardys had to stand—but they didn't mind. They rested the bags of books on the floor near their feet, and talked about some of the places they wanted to visit when they were in Kenya.

"I saw some great things in that shop that I'd like to get Iola, but I want to get them in Africa," Joe said.

"Yeah! I think Callie would like some African

jewelry," Frank said. Callie Shaw was Frank's best girlfriend in Bayport, although they really hadn't talked about any dates beyond the next prom. "But I want to get it in Africa, too. At least now, though, I have an idea of what to expect."

Joe was looking out the window as the train pulled into a station. "This is Middletown Road Station," he said. "One more stop before Pelham Bay Park."

Chet and his aunt Joyce were circling the block in his borrowed convertible. He saw the Hardy boys from the corner, whipped expertly into the no-parking zone in front of the subway entrance, and Frank and Joe jumped into the backseat.

"See! This was no problem at all," Chet said. "Everything went off without a hitch."

Frank and Joe grinned at each other. They decided to wait until the appearance of tomorrow morning's newspaper before they gave Chet a full account of their *uneventful* day.

The next day was unbelievably hectic. It started out with Chet showing up at the Hardys' front door just in time for breakfast, with a copy of *The New York Times* under his arm.

"What's the meaning of this?" Chet demanded. He had circled a story on the front page. "You guys helped to break up a big purse snatching ring, and you didn't tell me about it?"

Frank and Joe grinned at each other.

"What's to tell?" Joe said. "It was all in a day's work."

"How many pancakes would you like, Chet?" Mrs. Hardy asked.

"Oh, I'll take whatever's left," Chet said.

"Don't your parents ever feed you?" Aunt Gertrude asked.

Everyone in Bayport accepted the fact that Fenton Hardy's sister said exactly what was on her mind—and she didn't spare the Hardys her honesty, either. In fact, most of the time, it was Frank and Joe who were the objects of her acerbic remarks. Despite this, they loved her dearly and teased her unmercifully. Their aunt's remarks never angered them.

Chet went back to complaining that he didn't appreciate having to read a newspaper—and an out-of-town one at that!—to find out what his best friends were doing.

"Seriously, Chet, we really didn't know what a big deal it was," Frank admitted. "We just weren't going to let those punks get away with stealing that woman's purse."

"We didn't want to sound like we were bragging in front of your aunt, either," Joe said. "We decided just to let her think that you were more wonderful than we were."

"Thanks, guys," Chet said, rolling his eyes.

After breakfast some of the rest of the Hardys' friends arrived to help them get ready for the trip.

Iola was moping around, teary-eyed, until Joe finally said, "Look, Iola, we'll be back before you know it. It's not like we're leaving Bayport forever."

"I know, I know," Iola assured him. "I'm sorry."

Frank had to assure Callie of the same thing.

At lunchtime Mrs. Hardy and Aunt Gertrude interrupted the preparations with some sandwiches, chips, and sodas. By midafternoon, they were finished packing.

"Our plane leaves Kennedy at eight P.M. It's a direct flight to Nairobi with one stop in Dakar," Mr. Hardy said. "Chief Collig will be by in about an hour to take us to the airport."

Ezra Collig was the chief of the Bayport Police Department and a good friend of the Hardys. He had offered to take them to the airport, since he had to be in Queens for an evening appointment anyway. Frank and Joe thought it might also be because Chief Collig wanted to pick their father's brain about a case he was working on. Many of the crimes in Bayport were solved after Chief Collig made a visit to Fenton Hardy.

"I don't care what time it is here when you get to Kenya," Mrs. Hardy said. "I want you to call me and let me know that you arrived safely."

"We will, Mom," Frank assured his mother. "But don't worry. We'll be fine."

Chief Collig arrived promptly at the arranged time. Frank and Joe and their friends helped pack the police van Chief Collig was driving. They were taking two suitcases and one carry-on bag each.

Frank and Joe hugged their mother and said good-bye to their friends, promising to send post-cards—even though they knew they'd probably beat the postcards back to Bayport.

They each gave Aunt Gertrude a peck on the cheek. "When you show up at Kennedy in that police van, people will think you're convicts who are being deported," she said.

"Hey! That might be to our advantage," Joe said. "Maybe nobody will want to sit next to us, and we'll have more room to stretch out."

"You need to care more about your reputation than you do about sleeping," Aunt Gertrude said.

Joe grinned at her and gave her another peck on the cheek. He loved pushing his Aunt Gertrude's buttons.

"We need to go," Chief Collig warned them. "The traffic will be heavy as it is."

Mr. Hardy got in beside Chief Collig, and Frank and Joe climbed in the back.

They headed down High Street toward the

expressway that would take them to JFK Airport.

Frank and Joe had been right. Chief Collig was having trouble solving a case involving one of Bayport's leading businessmen. Some new information had come to light about the man, and Chief Collig wanted Fenton Hardy's opinion of how it should be handled.

Normally the Hardy boys would have listened to all of the conversation. The case didn't happen to be as interesting to them as the upcoming trip to Africa, though, and that's what the brothers spent the bulk of the drive talking about. By the time they arrived at the international terminal, they had made so many plans, they weren't sure if they'd have any time in Africa to sleep.

Aunt Gertrude had been partially right about the way people would react to the van. The police vehicle did raise a few eyebrows, but no one seemed really concerned. Once they had removed their luggage, the Hardys said good-bye to Chief Collig and headed into the terminal toward the check-in for Kenya International Airways.

"I'm glad there's this new, more direct flight," Mr. Hardy said. "If we had to go through Europe, it would take almost eight hours longer."

One at a time they presented their passports and tickets, checked their luggage, and got their boarding passes.

It took them several minutes to get through security, which was very tight. Joe even had to take off his shoes for careful inspection.

Once through security, Mr. Hardy looked at his watch. "I'm hungry. I've been so busy today that I didn't take time to eat much, and it'll be a while after we're airborne before we're served dinner. What about you boys?"

Joe shrugged. "Maybe a snack," he said.

Frank looked at some of the restaurants just down the hall from where they were standing. "I'm not starved, either, but I could probably eat something."

They finally decided on one of the fast food restaurants.

After Frank and Joe had finished their hamburgers and fries, they decided that maybe they should eat a second burger, too, in case the flight was delayed and dinner wasn't served until late.

Just as they were each finishing their second hamburger and had considered going for a third one, their flight was announced.

"That's us," Mr. Hardy said. "Let's go."

They threw their trash in a garbage pail on the way out of the restaurant and headed toward Gate 43 for their flight to Nairobi.

Just as they passed Gate 42 someone rushed passed them, bumping Frank out of the way.

"Hey!" Frank said. "Watch it!"

Joe stopped walking. "Frank! Look!" he whispered. "That's Jackson! The guy from Fifth Avenue Africana!"

The Hardy boys watched as Jackson stopped at Gate 43 to get in line to board the flight to Nairobi.

3 Two of the Engines Are Gone!

"What's wrong?" Fenton Hardy asked.

Frank told him about the encounter with the man in Fifth Avenue Africana.

"We didn't mention it before, Dad, because it didn't seem all that important at the time," Joe added.

"Well, it may not even be important now. The man obviously has connections to Africa," Mr. Hardy said. "He would probably have a good reason for taking a flight to Kenya."

"Mr. Watson implied Jackson had offered to bring him mounted heads of big game," Frank said, "and even the skins of some animals in danger of extinction."

Fenton Hardy shook his head in dismay. "I can't believe there are *still* people around the world who think how they furnish their home is more important than the future of these endangered animals."

When they arrived at Gate 43, the Hardys got in line to board.

"I hope he's not sitting close to us," Joe whispered. "That face will give me nightmares."

Frank nodded his head in agreement.

Fortunately when they took their seats in first class, Jackson was nowhere in sight. Frank and Joe were sitting in side-by-side leather seats. Mr. Hardy was directly across the aisle. No one as yet was sitting in the window seat beside him.

A flight attendant dressed in what Joe thought might be native Kenyan attire handed them hot cloths.

"Oh, that feels good," Frank said, as he wiped his face and hands with the steaming cloth. He turned to Mr. Hardy. "I could get used to being pampered like this."

Mr. Hardy grinned. "Well, I figured that we'd be more rested if we flew first class. I didn't want us to be tired when we got there, and the eight-hour time difference will create enough problems as it is. I just hope I don't fall asleep in the middle of one of my talks."

The same flight attendant now was handing them some delicious-looking snacks and mango juice. "This will get you ready for our food in Kenya," she said in an accent.

"Great!" Joe said. "I'm starving."

Mr. Hardy looked across the aisle, raised an eyebrow in puzzlement, but didn't say anything.

Frank took a bite of one of the snacks. "Mmm!" he said. "What's this called?"

"Samosa," the flight attendant said. "It's deep-fried pastry filled with chopped meat and vegetables."

Just as the Hardy boys were finishing their second round of Kenyan snacks and fruit juice, the plane began taxiing for takeoff. They put their trays in the upright position and leaned back to enjoy the thrill they always got when a speeding plane forced them back into their seats.

"This must be how astronauts feel," Joe said as the Kenya International Airways plane raced down the runway. He put his hands on the armrests and pretended that he was heading to the moon.

"Yeah, I guess," Frank said.

Joe looked over at him. "What's the matter? You usually like takeoffs as much as I do."

"Nothing," Frank said. He didn't admit that he was preoccupied. For some reason, he was wondering what Jackson was thinking right now. In fact, he now wished that they were sitting close to him. He'd feel better if he could keep an eye on him all night.

The Hardy boys decided that flying first class was almost like having your own personal staff of flight attendants. Their attendant seemed to anticipate their every wish. She gave them handheld

27

video games to play and sports magazines to read while they waited for dinner.

Dinner itself was delicious. When Frank and Joe asked what each dish was called, they were given the Swahili names of the foods. One of the flight attendants gave Frank a Swahili phrase book.

"Here's a CD and player that you can listen to also," she said.

Instead of watching the movie, Frank studied tourist Swahili. When he was finished, he turned to Joe. "You should listen to this, too," Frank said to his brother. "You never know when the language might come in handy."

"They speak English in Kenya, too," Joe reminded him, "so I'll just stick to that."

"Typical attitude," Frank said.

"Okay, then I'll let you translate for me," Joe said.

Frank shook his head and decided to listen to the CD again. Joe was engrossed in the movie. It was one that Frank had taken Callie to see, and he wasn't particularly interested in seeing it again. He looked over at his father. Mr. Hardy's reading light was on, and he was poring over one of the books that Mr. Watson had lent him.

When the movie was over, the flight attendants turned down the lights and brought pillows and blankets for everyone. Some passengers, like Fenton Hardy, still had on their overhead lights—but each delivered only a narrow stream of illumination to the seat directly beneath it, so readers didn't disturb napping passengers nearby.

Frank stood up and started toward the restroom, but someone a couple of seats ahead got there first.

"It's all right if you want to use one of the others toward the back of the aircraft," one of the flight attendants told him.

"Oh, no, that's . . . ," Frank started to say, then changed his mind. "Well, if it's okay." It had suddenly occurred to him that this would be a great opportunity to check out where Jackson was seated.

He returned to his seat and told Joe what he was doing.

"I think I need to go, too, before I go to sleep, so I'll come with you," Joe said.

The curtain separating first class from the rest of the plane had already been drawn, but the Hardy boys parted it and headed toward the rear of the aircraft.

They were sure that the flight attendants wouldn't be watching them, so they decided it wouldn't really be necessary to stop at the first restroom. They wanted to locate exactly where Jackson was sitting.

The lights all over the aircraft had been dimmed, so the boys weren't noticed as they conducted their search.

"I don't know why this is so important to me," Frank whispered. "I'll just feel better if I know where he is, I guess."

"I agree," Joe said.

They passed one set of restrooms in the middle of the aircraft that were unoccupied, but continued toward the back of the plane. They found Jackson near the rear of the cabin. He was sitting on the aisle in the last row of seats. He seemed to be asleep, but the Hardy boys didn't take a chance. They passed him without looking too closely. Both restrooms were unoccupied so Frank used one, and Joe used the other.

When they finished, they stood together for a few seconds right behind Jackson's seat. They were close enough to hear a slight snoring noise, letting them know that he was asleep. Then they started back toward first class.

Mr. Hardy was just closing his book when Frank and Joe got to their seats. "I take it you two were on a reconnaissance mission," he said.

Frank nodded. "Subject is asleep at the rear of the plane," he said.

"Then I think that's probably what we should do," Mr. Hardy said. "You won't want to spend your first day in Nairobi in bed, right?"

Frank and Joe settled themselves into their comfortable seats, arranged their pillows and blankets, and turned out their lights.

In just a few minutes, they both drifted off to sleep.

* * * *

It was almost dawn when the flight attendants began awakening everyone for the landing in Dakar.

The aircraft was only on the ground long enough to refuel and take on a few passengers. The Hardy boys thought, from their formal appearances, that these people were businessmen and -women headed to Nairobi.

When the plane was airborne again, the flight attendants started serving breakfast. Frank was surprised to see an omelette, with hash browns and toast—much like a breakfast his mother would serve. This gave him a feeling of comfort.

The pilot announced that they had crossed the border of Senegal and were now over Mali.

Joe looked out the window. "Hey! I wonder if we'll be flying over Tombouctou," he said, naming the fabled city that was often used as a metaphor for faraway places.

Frank got a route map out of the seat pocket in front of him and handed it to Joe. "Check it out," he said.

After a few minutes of searching, Joe said, "It's probably too far north. It looks way out of the way."

"You never know, Joe," Frank said. "Pilots don't always fly in straight lines."

A consultation with a flight attendant who checked with the pilot proved that Joe was right. They would be flying south of Tombouctou.

Over the loudspeaker, the pilot informed everyone

that they were now flying over Bamako, the capital of Mali. He reminded the passengers that a route map was available in their seat pocket and that their flight path would pretty much follow it.

Joe could see that they would cross over Burkina Faso, Ghana, Togo, Benin, Nigeria, Cameroon, Central African Republic, Congo, Uganda, and then Kenya. Joe tried to remember the history of each of the countries that he had studied in class.

Later, just as the pilot announced that they were flying over Kampala, the capital of Uganda, the aircraft started shaking violently.

Several passengers screamed.

The Hardy boys looked at each other.

Frank swallowed hard. "I hope that was just turbulence," he whispered to Joe.

"Frank, I don't think it was," Joe said. He pointed out his window. "That engine is on fire."

Frank leaned over to get a closer look. Joe was right. Below them he could see only the green of the jungle.

"Boys, keep your seat belts fastened," Mr. Hardy called to his sons, "and listen carefully to any instructions that you're given."

Joe could see that his father had his cell phone in his hand. *Is he thinking of a way he can contact Mom and Aunt Gertrude?* he wondered. Joe's stomach was beginning to feel queasy.

Frank was thinking of some of the movies he'd

seen where planes crash landed in African jungles. Several people always survived, but they had a hard time coping—with each other, and unfriendly people they encountered in the jungle. *How much of that is true,* Frank wondered, *and how much of it is just Hollywood?*

There was a sudden crackling noise, and then the pilot's voice was on the loudspeaker. "We have lost one of our engines, and we've begun to lose altitude, but we think we can make it into Nairobi with the remaining engines. The flight attendants will be passing through the cabin, giving you instructions on what to do in case we have to make a forced landing."

The flight attendant who had just hours earlier been telling the Hardy boys all about the wonderful food in Kenya was now showing them how to hide their heads in pillows in their laps to protect them during a crash.

Frank couldn't help thinking it wouldn't do much good, because he was sure that a jet going as fast as they were going would be torn apart by all of the trees—but he wasn't going to express that opinion now. He had to hope that everything would be all right.

Joe was looking out his window. "So far so good on this side," he said. "Maybe we'll . . ."

At that moment a loud explosion shook the entire plane. It seemed to have come from Mr. Hardy's side of the cabin.

"Dad! Dad!" Joe shouted. "What happened?"

Mr. Hardy was looking out the window. When he turned around, Frank could see that his father's face was drained of all color. "We just lost another engine!" Mr. Hardy managed to say.

4 Danger over Africa

The plane began to fall rapidly. People were scream-ing and crying throughout the aircraft.

"Do you think that Jackson had something to do with this, Frank?" Joe whispered.

"What do you mean, Joe?" Frank said. "That he's *responsible* for what's happened? No."

"Well, if he didn't do it himself, then maybe he made somebody mad," Joe countered. "He's cer-tainly capable of doing that. Maybe this is all hap-pening because he's on board."

Frank hadn't considered that possibility, but it seemed remote, and he told Joe so. "No, I think it's our bad luck. I just hope we can make it into Nairobi on two engines."

"Ladies and gentlemen," the pilot's voice began

again. "The two remaining engines seem to be stabilized, and we're just thirty minutes out from Jomo Kenyatta International Airport in Nairobi." There was a loud cheer from the passengers.

The pilot didn't say anything for several seconds, and Joe knew they were in for some bad news. "But . . . ," the pilot began, to the groans of several people. "Our nose landing-gear unit seems to be stuck. If we can't get it unstuck, we'll have to try to make a landing on soft foam. We should be all right."

"I don't like the way he said 'should,'" Frank whispered to Joe.

"Me, either," Joe said. He looked over at Frank. "What could be making it stick?" he asked.

"Something could have come loose somewhere when the engines went out. It really shook the plane good," Frank said. "It could have fallen into the nose landing-gear unit."

He and Tony Prito had spent last summer working with Jack Wayne on a small jet Jack had bought at an auction. Jack was Fenton Hardy's charter pilot when Mr. Hardy needed to fly across the country while on cases. Frank and Tony had learned a lot about the inner workings of jets.

"So the solution could be as simple as removing it from the nose landing-gear unit," Joe said, "provided there was someone to do it."

"Forget it, guys," Fenton Hardy said. "That would be extremely dangerous."

"Dad! We're already in danger," Joe said. "There's no guarantee that when the nose of the plane hits the foam on the runway the aircraft won't break apart."

Fenton Hardy took a deep breath. "This is one of those times when I wish your mother and I hadn't reared two smart kids," he said. "I don't have a counterargument to your reasoning."

"Do you think the pilots would let us take a look, Dad?" Frank asked. "Jack showed me what to do last summer if something like this happened. He's had to do it before."

Mr. Hardy thought for a minute. "Well, we won't know until we ask them, will we?" he finally said.

Needless to say, the pilots didn't think it was a good idea, and initially refused the Hardy boys' request. At Fenton Hardy's insistence, though, they agreed to contact one of Mr. Hardy's most important acquaintances in Johannesburg, South Africa, who vouched for him, saying that if Fenton Hardy thought it was a good idea, then it was a good idea.

Below the carpet in first class there was a trapdoor that led down into the undercarriage. The retractable nose landing-gear unit was inside this space.

At Mr. Hardy's request, the flight attendants closed the curtain that separated first class from the rest of the cabins—so that none of the other passengers could see what was taking place.

"It's best that we not unnerve them any more than we have to at this point," Fenton Hardy explained.

"They might get nervous if they think two teenage boys are trying to solve this problem." He winked at his sons.

The Hardy boys quickly removed the carpet that covered the center aisle. Their father and one of the flight attendants helped them.

After the carpet was removed, it was rolled up and placed in one of the empty seats. It didn't take the Hardy boys long to open the trapdoor.

With flashlights in hand, the boys slowly began their descent into the belly of the plane.

"I'm glad I helped Jack work on his plane this past summer," Frank said. "This all looks really familiar. There's just more of it."

With Frank leading the way, the Hardy boys climbed deeper into the undercarriage of the nose of the airplane, toward the landing-gear unit. The noise was deafening, and the deeper they went, the colder it got.

"We're almost there," Frank shouted.

When Joe didn't respond, Frank pulled on his sleeve and pointed. He mouthed that they were almost there, and this time Joe understood him.

Joe shined the flashlight around the area. He could see some strips of metal dangling from the top of the ceiling, which was the underside of the floor of the first-class passenger cabin. He didn't know as much about this part of the aircraft as Frank did, but he did know enough to realize that whatever had happened to the engines had probably also caused this damage.

"Shine the flashlight down here," Frank called. He also motioned his instructions with his hands.

Joe did as Frank asked.

"I see the problem," Frank said, enunciating his words so his lips could be read. "One of those strips of metal fell into the cavity and wrapped around the gears. They won't move because of that." Slowly, Frank lowered himself onto the landing gear to reach the foreign object. When he tried to remove it, though, it was stuck tight. "I can't find the end of the metal strip to get any leverage," he shouted up to Joe. "When the captain tested the landing gear for landing in Nairobi, I think that must have caused this stuff to become wedged even more tightly."

"Do you think we can lower the gear manually?" Joe asked.

"That's what we'll have to do," Frank replied. He thought for a minute. "You'd better climb back up and tell Dad. He needs to tell the captain not to use his controls to try to lower the landing gear. I don't want to be working on them if that happens."

"Okay," Joe shouted.

While Joe climbed back up to relay the message to the pilot, Frank set to work seeing if he could release the landing gear manually. He knew from working with Jack Wayne approximately where the gear handle was that would allow him to do it. When he found the handle, he tried to turn it with one hand while holding the flashlight with the other, but it wouldn't budge. It was going to take both his hands and probably even Joe's to turn it.

A light from above told Frank that Joe was returning from delivering the message to the pilot.

"One more problem," Joe shouted when he reached Frank's side.

"What?" Frank asked.

"We're running low on fuel," Joe yelled.

"We just refueled in Dakar, Joe," Frank told him. "How could we be running low on fuel?"

"Well, it's just one of those things that passengers are never told, Frank," Joe replied. "It seems that the fuel reserves are low at Dakar, for some reason, and airplanes are only being given enough fuel to make it to their destinations."

"You're kidding me," Frank said.

"Nope. It's true. They know how long it takes to fly from Dakar to Nairobi, so that's how much fuel we got. Not a drop more," Joe said. "In other words, the pilot can't circle the airport until we get the landing gear unstuck."

"Listen, Joe, here's how this plane works," Frank shouted. "Without the front landing gear down, the plane will hit the ground nose first. Bad angle. It would be better if we had lost the main landing gear, because at least that way, the front of the plane would be elevated."

"I see what you mean," Joe said. He took a deep breath. "Well, let's get to work. This won't be the place to be when we hit the runway."

Joe found a place that would hold their flashlights securely and still give them the light they needed to see as they tried to unstick the landing gears. Together they pushed on` the manual handle—but it still wouldn't budge.

"I've got to get underneath the wheels to find the end of the metal strip," Frank said. "That'll mean standing on the retractable doors, which is kind of dangerous. But I don't know what else to do."

Joe knew that if for some reason the doors happened to open with Frank standing on them, his brother would fall several thousand feet to the jungle below.

Slowly Frank made his way underneath the landing gear. He stepped tentatively onto the nose gear flaps, making sure that most of the pressure remained in his upper body rather than in his legs.

He used his flashlight to search the area for the end of the metal strip. He was just about to give up when he spotted it.

"I found it, Joe!" Frank shouted above to his brother.

"Can you get it out?" Joe shouted down to him.

"I think so," Frank shouted back.

There was no good place to lay the flashlight so

Frank held it under his arm, freeing his hand to try to remove the strip of metal. He could budge it but he still couldn't free it.

"Hey, Joe!" Frank shouted. "Use the manual handle, but this time, turn it the other way. I think that'll work."

"Okay, Frank," Joe shouted.

Above, Joe grasped the handle with both hands, and using all the strength he could muster, began to turn it. It started to move very slowly.

Suddenly the lever turned several inches and a great rush of freezing air filled the undercarriage.

"Frank! Frank!" Joe shouted.

Frantically Joe tried to turn the lever in the other direction, but now it was moving of its own accord. Joe didn't have the strength to stop it.

Below, Frank had just grasped one of the wheels when his foot fell through the opening flaps.

"Joe! Joe!" Frank shouted. "Close the flaps!"

Even as he said it, Frank knew that Joe couldn't hear him. Besides, he was still able to reason, his brother knew enough to do that anyway. If it wasn't happening, it was because Joe couldn't do it.

Now the landing gear itself began to lower—and Frank with it. In just a few seconds, he was outside the airplane, dangling from the wheels. The fierce, icy winds were whipping his body unmercifully. Frank's grasp on the wheel—and on his life—was tentative at best.

Frank still had enough wits about him to know that the only way he was going to get back inside the body of the plane was by pulling himself up. Against the incredibly strong winds, he managed to lift his head.

He squinted his eyes to protect them from the blasts of frigid air. Suddenly he saw Joe.

Frank knew Joe was saying something to him, because he could see his mouth working. There was no way he could make out what it was. Then he saw something in Joe's hand. It looked like a piece of rope.

Somehow Joe had been able to . . .

Frank blinked. For a moment he was sure that beside Joe, he had seen his father. Yes! Together they had managed to secure a rope to something inside the plane. He might make it after all.

Joe was shouting something at him. Just then the rope dropped in front of him, but the wind started whipping it back and forth, so that he couldn't grab it. He didn't know how much longer he could hold on to the wheels, either. He could no longer feel his hands. They were almost frozen. The rope continued to whip around him, several times slapping at his face, causing an almost unbearable sting. It reminded him of cold winter days in Bayport, when he was a kid, playing outside with his brother. When Mrs. Hardy told them it was time to come in, he remembered the stinging sensation as the warmth began to return to his face and hands.

Suddenly the rope disappeared. Frank looked up and squinted. What was happening? Had they given up?

No! Joe was going to lower the rope again—this time, Frank hoped, closer to where he was.

Frank grasped the wheel tighter. Was it just his imagination, Frank wondered, or were the winds less strong now? He glanced below and thought that the ground seemed closer. Then he could see houses, roads, and even vehicles.

Frank swallowed hard. They had reached Nairobi. He knew that there wasn't enough fuel for them to circle the city. The pilot had to land the plane as soon as possible.

5 The Shopkeeper in Mombasa Curios

There was no way that Joe Hardy was going to let anything happen to his brother. He had a plan, which Fenton Hardy at first vetoed. When Joe pleaded with his father, telling him that this might be the only way they could save Frank, Fenton Hardy finally relented. In fact, he let it be known that he couldn't have been prouder of Joe for being willing to risk his own life for his brother.

One of the copilots had now joined them in the undercarriage. He brought with him some dire news.

"We'll be on the ground in about five minutes," he said. "We've got to get your son back into the undercarriage."

Joe knew what the pilot wasn't saying. Even though

it made him angry, he tried to understand. If they had to wait any longer for them to get Frank inside the plane, there wouldn't be enough fuel for a safe landing. They couldn't take that chance. If it meant sacrificing one person to save the rest of the passengers, well . . .

That's not going to happen! Joe decided.

"Tie this rope around my waist, Dad," Joe said, "and then lower me to where I can grab Frank."

Together Mr. Hardy and the copilot secured the rope around Joe's waist and slowly lowered him down to where Frank was still hanging precariously by one of the plane's wheels.

Nothing had prepared Joe for the fierce winds that buffeted him. They began whipping him back and forth, continually bumping him against Frank and the landing gear. Joe was concerned that this might cause Frank to lose his grip and fall, but somehow, through it all, Frank still managed to hold on.

Quickly Joe decided that the only way this was going to work would be for Frank to grab Joe around the waist the next time the winds slammed Joe against the landing gear.

Joe pantomimed to Frank what he wanted him to do. Frank nodded that he understood.

As if the fates were against them, the wind now seemed to pull Joe in every direction except toward

Frank. Joe looked below him and could tell that they were getting even closer to the ground. In fact, now he could see the runways of Jomo Kenyatta International Airport.

Finally, just as the plane began turning, Joe slammed up against the landing gear and Frank grabbed him around his waist. They swung wildly for several seconds, then they began rising toward the landing-gear flaps. Fenton Hardy and the copilot struggled to get the boys inside the aircraft.

Finally they made it to the flaps of the landing gear. They were safe.

"Hold on!" the copilot shouted.

At that moment the wheels of the plane hit the runway, sending a choking smoke into the undercarriage.

Frank could hardly breathe. Almost as fast as the smoke had covered them, it disappeared. The Hardy boys lay still on the cold metal and covered their ears as the pilot put the engines in reverse to slow the plane.

When the aircraft had slowed enough to allow them to stand up, Frank and Joe, along with the copilot and Mr. Hardy, made their way back up into the first-class compartment—to the cheers of their fellow passengers in first class.

One of the flight attendants was waiting for them with blankets and hot beverages.

The Hardy boys accepted everyone's thanks and took big gulps of their hot chocolate.

"This is the best stuff I've ever tasted," Joe said.

Frank glanced out the window and shivered. He didn't know if it was because he was still chilled or because he was thinking about what could have happened if his hands had slipped off the tire.

By the time the aircraft reached the gate, the first-class cabin had been returned, more or less, to its original condition.

Frank and Joe had also recovered enough that they felt they could deplane normally, although information about what had happened had been radioed ahead to the Kenyan authorities and they had informed the pilot that medical personnel would be waiting for them at the arrival gate. They wanted to make sure the famous Fenton Hardy and his sons were all right.

Frank and Joe insisted that this was unnecessary, but Mr. Hardy said, "I think it's best that we allow the Kenyan authorities to examine you. They feel a certain responsibility to make sure you're okay, boys. Also, they probably want to express their gratitude."

Frank and Joe just hoped that everything would be kept low-key. When they walked down the gangway and saw newspaper and television reporters waiting for them, they resigned themselves to a fuss.

"So much for anonymity," Frank said to Joe under

his breath. "Now we won't be able to go anywhere in Kenya without people recognizing us."

An official-looking man rushed up to them. "This way, please!" he said.

He ushered the Hardy boys and their father to a room close by. Besides medical staff, several government ministers were in the room.

"The government of Kenya thanks you," one of the ministers told the Hardy boys. "If it weren't for your bravery, we could have lost several of our citizens, as well as citizens from other countries."

Frank and Joe accepted the thanks with their usual modesty.

"If there's anything that we can do to make your stay in Kenya more enjoyable, all you need to do is call my office," another minister said. He handed his card to Frank.

"Thank you, sir," Frank said. He pocketed the card immediately. *You can never tell,* he thought. *It's nice to have friends in high places.*

The medical staff agreed with Frank and Joe's earlier prognosis. The Hardy boys really were in good shape, physically and mentally, especially considering the harrowing experience they had been through.

"We work out daily and try to eat right," Joe told them. "It paid off today."

Frank nodded. "I'll never complain again when

coach makes us do extra push-ups," he said. "I know that's where I got the strength today to hang on to those tires."

A representative from the Kenya National Police Organization was waiting for the Hardys when they left the lounge. He introduced himself as Lieutenant John Kitale.

"I apologize, Mr. Hardy," Lieutenant Kitale said. "There was an accident on the way to the airport that tied up traffic, and I was late getting here." He looked at Frank and Joe. "I've already been informed of your heroism. You're to be congratulated. I'm just glad that everyone is safe."

"Thank you," Frank and Joe said as they shook hands with Lieutenant Kitale.

"I have a car waiting just outside the main entrance," the lieutenant said.

With Kitale in the lead, they cleared customs in minutes. Frank and Joe couldn't help but notice all of the admiring looks they got.

Just as they rounded a corner that would lead them to the main lobby of the terminal, Joe grabbed Frank by the arm and stopped. Lieutenant Kitale and Mr. Hardy were in front of them, engrossed in a conversation about the police department.

"Look over there, Frank," Joe said. He nodded to his right. "Do you see anybody you recognize?"

Frank looked. "Jackson!" he said.

Jackson was in a heated telephone conversation with someone.

"I wish I could listen," Joe said.

"Yeah," Frank agreed. "We could probably learn a lot."

"Boys!" Frank and Joe looked over to see Mr. Hardy and Lieutenant Kitale waiting for them. "We need to get into town."

The Hardy boys hurried to catch up.

As Lieutenant Kitale had said, a police department vehicle with plenty of flashing lights was waiting for them in front of the terminal. The four of them got into the back, and the driver pulled out into traffic.

Several people in front of the terminal stopped to look. Frank and Joe grinned at each other. They were certainly making a grand entrance into Nairobi, they thought.

When they left Jomo Kenyatta International Airport, they turned right onto the Mombasa Highway that would take them into central Nairobi.

Mr. Hardy had made reservations for them at the New Stanley Hotel, because he and Mrs. Hardy had once spent time there, right after they were married, and Mr. Hardy had fond memories of their stay. The conference was being held at the Hilton Hotel, which was only three blocks away, and Mr. Hardy said he wouldn't mind the walk.

When they arrived in front of the New Stanley

Hotel, the manager and several members of the staff were waiting for them.

The New Stanley's lobby seemed small and dark and kind of crowded to the Hardy boys, given the size of the hotel itself. The walls were paneled in dark wood, and the furnishings were dark leather. There was a lively feel about the place, though, with people coming and going.

Within minutes they were in their room.

"So far, I like this place!" Frank said as he collapsed onto the bed he had chosen.

"Who wouldn't?" Joe said. He looked around. "Anyone for food? I'm starved."

"Let's have something sent up, boys," Mr. Hardy suggested. "I'm hungry, too, but I want to unpack, check over some of my material for my lectures, and call your mother." He thought for a minute. "On second thought, maybe we'd better call your mother and Aunt Gertrude first. If they heard what happened from watching the news, they'll be really upset."

"Good idea, Dad," Frank agreed. "Knowing Aunt Gertrude, she'd be on the next plane to Nairobi."

Joe rolled his eyes. "I don't think Africa is ready for Aunt Gertrude," he said.

Frank laughed. "Would you mind if Joe and I ate in the Thorn Tree Café, Dad? You told us it's pretty good."

"That sounds like a super idea. Your mother and I loved it," Mr. Hardy said. "You might as well get your trip started. I'm going to be plenty busy, so you won't want to keep waiting on me to do things."

The Hardy boys took turns in the bathroom, rested for about a half hour, then dressed and headed for the Thorn Tree Café. They were seated at once, ahead of a couple who had been in front of them—but since the couple didn't seem to mind, Joe didn't bother to protest for them. Obviously the name "Hardy" was already opening doors in Kenya, just as it did in the United States.

In the center of the café there was a live thorn tree, from which the café got its name. Its huge branches acted as a sort of canopy. To the trunk of the tree, as was the tradition, were attached messages from various guests to other expected guests. Some of the messages had been there for years. The tradition dated from an earlier time, when Kenya was a British colony. Then almost everyone who came to Nairobi stayed at the New Stanley Hotel, and, because of the scarcity of telephones and other means of communication, this was about the only way to get information to friends.

"Today you can use cell phones," Joe remarked. "The world has seen a lot of changes."

The Hardy boys looked over the menu, then

decided to take a chance on what the waiter suggested.

He suggested *mushkaki*, small pieces of grilled and marinated meat off the skewer. With it, they had *ndizi*—plantains, and *maharagwe*—red kidney beans cooked with coconut.

Just as they were finishing, Joe looked up and saw Jackson strolling down the sidewalk.

The Hardy boys looked at each other and nodded.

Frank quickly signed the check, leaving a generous tip, and they left the café to follow Jackson.

Jackson turned at Mama Ngina Street and headed toward Moi Avenue, the main thoroughfare of central Nairobi.

Even though the street was crowded, the Hardy boys had no problem keeping Jackson in sight. After two more blocks, he turned into the doorway of a small shop. When the Hardy boys reached the shop, they read the sign above the door: MOMBASA CURIOS.

Frank gave Joe a puzzled look. "He doesn't look like the type of person who'd be buying souvenirs," he said.

Joe nodded. "I say we check it out."

When they entered Mombasa Curios, a bell jangled above the door. The shop was typical of its kind, with shelves full of wooden masks, carved animals, blankets, and various kinds of beaded work. Most of it looked relatively inexpensive.

After several minutes, when no one appeared, Frank called, "Is there anybody here?"

A door opened at the back of the shop, and an elderly Indian man appeared.

Joe had a sense of déjà vu from Fifth Avenue Africana.

"I'm sorry. I was unpacking some goods in the back. I didn't hear you," the man said. "Things have been very slow today. In fact, you're the first people who have even come into the shop."

The boys looked at each other.

Why was this man lying to them? Frank wondered.

6 Riot!

"Well, we'll just look around then, if you don't mind," Frank said. "We have a lot of gifts to buy, and we want to make sure we pick out the right ones."

"Of course," the man said. He began busying himself at the counter. "Call me if you need any assistance."

The Hardy boys made a complete circle of the shop, pretending to browse.

"I know that Jackson came in here," Joe whispered. "He has to be somewhere in this shop."

"He's probably in that back room," Frank whispered. "We have to think up a way to distract the shopkeeper, so one of us can slip inside."

They continued to look at the goods on the shelves.

Joe actually liked some of the animal carvings. He made a quick calculation of American dollars to Kenyan shillings and realized that the carvings weren't all that expensive. If he didn't find any he liked better, he'd probably come back to this shop before they left and buy some of them.

After the Hardy boys had made a third pass through the shop, the Indian shopkeeper looked up and gave them what Frank thought was an unfriendly glance.

"He's probably going to ask us to leave soon," Joe whispered. "We're keeping him from doing whatever business he was doing with Jackson."

Suddenly Joe had an idea. He walked over to the shopkeeper. "I really like your shop," he said. "It reminds me of one we visited in New York City."

"Really?" the man said. He suddenly seemed nervous. "What's the name of the New York shop?"

"Fifth Avenue Africana," Frank replied.

The man stared at them for several seconds without saying anything. Then, just as he opened his mouth, they heard chants and shouting on the street.

"Oh, not again!" the man groaned. "Not again!"

He ran to his shop window. Frank and Joe followed.

"What's going on?" Joe asked.

"It's the farmers and the animal rights people. They don't like each other very much," the man said. He looked exasperated. "I wish they'd settle their differences."

"What are their differences?" Frank asked.

"The farmers want more land. They want the government to take some of the land reserved for the wild animals so they can plant their crops on it," the man said. "The animal rights people are against it. They say the animals already don't have enough land to exist on."

Just then a brick came flying through the shop window, covering the shop owner with small pieces of glass and just barely missing the boys.

The shop owner brushed the glass off, then flew out the door of the shop into the crowd.

"Joe—now's our chance!" Frank said. "We can see what's in that back room."

Quickly the Hardy boys raced to the rear of the shop. Just as Frank opened the door, he saw someone leaving by another door at the back of the storage room.

"It's Jackson!" Joe said.

They started running.

Right before they got to the door to the outside, the shopkeeper shouted, "You have no right to be back here. I'm going to call the police. I'll have you arrested."

Quickly Joe pushed on the door. It opened onto an alley. "There he is!"

Jackson was already at the end of the alley, heading toward the crowd of demonstrators on Moi Avenue.

The boys raced after him. But by the time they reached Moi Avenue, Jackson had disappeared in the throng.

"What now?" Joe asked.

Before Frank could answer, someone thrust a sign into his hands.

"You can't demonstrate without a sign," a girl shouted at him. "It isn't allowed."

"But we're not really . . . ," Frank started to say.

"You're not really what?" the girl demanded. "You're not really in favor of keeping the animals in Kenya alive?"

"No, no, it's not that," Joe intervened. "It's just that—"

"I know you. I saw your faces on television," the girl interrupted him. "You're the Hardy boys from America. You saved all those passengers on the Kenya International Airways flight from New York this morning."

Before Frank and Joe could tell the girl that she was right, a shoving match began—and Frank and Joe and the girl were in the middle of it. They were all getting battered with opposition signs.

"People have to eat! They're more important!" a demonstrator shouted. "Animals don't need the best land."

"They're important, too!" Joe shouted back. "We can't let African animals die out!"

That set off two more of the opposition demonstrators. They started battering Joe with their placards.

Somewhere in the distance, Joe thought he heard the sound of police whistles.

Suddenly he felt himself being pulled out of the crowd. There was such mass confusion that none of the opposition demonstrators seemed to notice that he was leaving.

When Joe finally looked at who was pulling him, he saw Frank and the girl on the sidewalk. They all crouched behind a parked car.

"Thanks!" Joe said. "I guess I got carried away."

The girl smiled. "Well, at least you found out what we're up against," she said. She held out her hand. "I'm Lilly Mtito. I'm a student at the University of Kenya."

The Hardy boys shook hands with her.

"We're having another rally on campus," Lilly said. "Would you care to come?"

"After all of this?" Frank said. "You mean the police will allow it?"

"Oh, yes. These demonstrations are a weekly event in Nairobi. The police don't interfere too much. They more or less let us take out our frustrations on each other," Lilly said. "Of course, they'll step in if things get really out of hand, but they know it's important for each side to vent its anger at the other, and they don't consider hitting someone on the head with a placard to be much of a crime."

Frank looked at Joe. "I'd like to find out more about the plight of the wild animals in Kenya," he said. "Dad will be busy putting the final preparations on his talk, so he won't want us disturbing him. How about it?"

Joe nodded. "And when we get back to Bayport, we can—"

"Lilly! Lilly! The farmers have Professor Makadara!" a voice shouted. They turned to see a slender young man running their way. When he reached them, out of breath, he continued, "They're beating him up. They blame him for everything!"

"Joseph! How could they? He's an old man!" Lilly cried. She looked at Frank and Joe. "Professor Makadara is one of the most respected educators in Kenya!"

Without waiting to be asked to help, Frank and Joe followed Lilly and Joseph back into the crowd on Moi Avenue. A block away, they saw two men with what looked like bicycle chains whipping another man who was lying on the street. The man was curled up, trying to keep his head and face covered. Joe could see that the chains had drawn blood.

In the distance he heard the wail of a police siren. Joe knew it was headed in their direction.

Frank and Joe dove at the men's backs, causing them to buckle to the ground. Lilly and the young man picked up the bicycle chains and shook them threateningly.

The police sirens were getting closer.

"You have to help us get Professor Makadara out of here," Lilly said frantically. "The police will arrest him. He's wanted for questioning."

Joe began to wonder just what he and Frank had gotten themselves into. He picked up the professor's legs, Frank grabbed the professor under his arms, and they quickly carried him in the direction that Lilly and Joseph were headed.

They wound their way through back alleys and several dimly lit shops, where no one seemed to think there was anything unusual about the Hardy boys carrying a bleeding elderly man.

Finally just when Joe thought he couldn't go any farther, they entered a covered passage that smelled of rotting garbage and stopped in front of a scarred wooden door.

Lilly took a key from one of her pockets, inserted it into the ancient lock, and opened the door.

Once inside, she lit a lamp, allowing the Hardy boys to see where they were: the professor's apartment.

Joe looked around. There were books stacked everywhere. Faded prints of some of the magnificent wildlife of Kenya adorned the walls.

"We need to put him to bed," Lilly said. "Bring him this way."

The professor's bedroom was at the back of the small apartment. Frank and Joe laid him gently on the bed.

"We'll need hot water, Joseph," Lilly said. "The kettle is on the stove. Please get it ready."

Joseph left the bedroom to do what Lilly had asked.

"Is there anything that we can do?" Joe asked.

Lilly had begun to undo the professor's shirt. "Well, yes, you can check the medicine cabinet in the bathroom," she said. "Bring whatever salves you can find."

But before the Hardy boys could react to Lilly's request, there was a loud pounding on the door.

"Police!" a voice shouted. "Open up!"

"Oh, no!" Lilly moaned. She looked at Frank and Joe. "They can't find you here. They won't believe you're not involved. You have to forget what you've seen!" She nodded toward the window. "Out that way! Just start running!"

"What about you?" Frank asked.

"I'm not going to leave Professor Makadara," Lilly said. "Now, go!"

In the front of the apartment, Frank and Joe could hear the door splinter. They raced to the window, opened it, and climbed out onto the ground. Lilly was standing there to close the window after them and to pull the curtains. With luck, no one would know they had been there.

"As much as I'd like to help," Frank said to Joe as they raced down the alley, "I don't think I'm ready to spend several years in a Kenyan jail."

"I wonder what Lilly meant, that Professor Makadara was wanted for questioning," Joe said.

"Maybe he's some sort of a fanatic, Joe," Frank replied. "We probably believe in some of the same things he believes in, but we follow the laws in our country. I'm thinking that maybe he didn't."

Without Lilly and Joseph leading the way for them, Frank and Joe had no idea where they were headed. Now people who hadn't paid any attention to them before were giving them strange looks. The Hardy boys weren't sure they were in a part of Nairobi where people cared about the Hardy name.

Frank and Joe quickened their pace and soon reached a street. A sign identified it as Haile Selassie Avenue. For a moment they didn't know which direction to take. Joe thought that going left would get them back to the hotel. It turned out that he was right. It led them back to Moi Avenue. Just as they were about to cross, a police car sped by, forcing them to jump back onto the sidewalk.

"Lilly!" Frank called.

Joe looked around. "Where?" he asked.

"In that police car. I'm sure it was her," Frank

said. "She had her face pressed against the window, looking in our direction."

"Lilly was worried that they were going to arrest Professor Makadara," Joe said. "I wonder why they arrested her."

"We need to talk to Dad about this, Joe," Frank said. "Maybe he can think of some way we can help Lilly, or at least figure out why this happened."

They crossed Moi Avenue and headed to the New Stanley Hotel. As they entered the lobby, they saw Jackson standing at the reception desk.

The Hardy boys ducked into the gift shop.

"I don't like this," Joe said. "Every time we see him, there's trouble!"

"I know," Frank agreed.

From where they were, they could see the reception area. The desk clerk who had been talking to Jackson looked at the mailboxes, then shook his head. Jackson stood for a minute, obviously thinking about something, then turned and left the hotel.

Frank and Joe went to the reception desk to get the key to their room.

"Ah, it's you," the desk clerk said. "You just missed your friend from America."

Frank gave the desk clerk a puzzled look. "Did he give you a name?"

"No. He said you didn't know he was coming," the desk clerk said. "He said he had a big surprise for you."

65

7 Poachers on the Loose

The Hardy boys decided to take the stairs to their room, rather than wait for the elevators in the crowded lobby.

"I'm not sure I want to know what kind of surprise he has for us," Joe said.

"I know," Frank said. He thought for a minute. "Lilly saw our pictures on television. That's how she knew us," he added. "Jackson doesn't strike me as the kind who'd spend much time watching television. He must have been watching us from the door of the shop."

"You're right, Frank. I don't really think he knew we were on the plane. We pretty much kept out of sight," Joe said. "He probably recognized us from

Fifth Avenue Africana and is now wondering what we're doing here."

They had reached their floor and turned down the corridor toward the room. Frank and Joe had already decided that they wouldn't bother their father with the new information about Jackson. They were used to taking care of themselves in situations like this.

Fenton Hardy had dozed off, sitting in an armchair with one of his speeches on his lap. He woke up, though, when the boys entered the room.

"I take it you've been seeing the sights," Mr. Hardy said.

"Yup," Frank said. "We took a little tour of the area."

"Did you get a lot of work done, Dad?" Joe asked.

Fenton Hardy nodded. "Surprisingly, yes," he replied.

"Why 'surprisingly,' Dad?" Frank asked.

"The telephone has been ringing off the hook. I think every journalist in Kenya wants to interview you," Mr. Hardy explained. "You're quite the heroes!"

Joe yawned. "Do you think they'll call back? I want to go to bed."

"I don't think so," Mr. Hardy said. "By now, you're probably old news."

"Well, we were almost new news again," Frank said. "We got caught in a demonstration between the farmers and the animal rights activists on Moi Avenue."

Joe nodded. "The farmers were beating up an elderly professor—an animal rights activist. We met a girl named Lilly Mtito who needed help carrying him to his apartment. But then the police came and took Lilly and the professor away."

"Joe and I made sure the professor was safely hidden, then escaped through a bedroom window," Frank said. "Lilly didn't want us to get arrested."

Fenton Hardy seemed to study the situation for a minute. "Was this man's name Makadara?" he asked.

"Yes!" Joe exclaimed. "How did you know?"

Mr. Hardy let out a big sigh. "Well, Professor Makadara may mean well, boys, but he's created a lot of problems for the Kenyan government."

"How so, Dad?" Frank asked.

"It's a difficult problem to solve, and the government is really trying to appease both sides," Mr. Hardy said. "They know that with an expanding population, the farmers will need more land on which to grow crops—but they also know how important it is to ensure the survival of the wildlife, not only for environmental reasons, but for economic reasons. The tourist industry is very important to Kenya, and most tourists come here to see the wild animals."

"But how does Professor Makadara fit in to this?" Joe asked.

"Unfortunately, Professor Makadara sees only one side of the issue," Fenton Hardy said. "He's been accused of destroying a lot of farmers' property. I've received several reports on him from the Kenya police. They've never been able to prove anything, but they feel they're close."

"I can't believe that Lilly would do anything like that," Joe said.

"Me, either," Frank agreed. "We were wondering . . ."

". . . if I could find out what the situation is with her," Fenton Hardy finished the sentence.

Frank nodded.

Mr. Hardy dialed a number and asked to be connected to Lieutenant Kitale. After a few minutes the conversation ended, and Mr. Hardy hung up the phone. He told his sons that Professor Makadara would be put on trial for his crimes, but that Lilly Mtito had been released. The Hardy boys felt bad for the professor, but they were glad to learn that Lilly was going to be all right.

"I'll be busy all day tomorrow with the opening sessions of the conference," Mr. Hardy said, "so I took the liberty of arranging a trip to the Nairobi National Park for you. I hope that's okay. You didn't have anything definite in mind to do, did you?"

Frank and Joe shook their heads.

"That sounds like a great idea," Frank said.

"Well, this will let you see some of Kenya's wildlife

69

up close. The park is just a few miles outside the city. It won't take very long to get there, but it'll feel the same as if you were farther out in the bush. Your mother and I loved it there."

"When do we leave?" Joe asked.

"Kind of early," Mr. Hardy said. "You need to be at the hotel entrance at four—A.M."

The Hardy boys groaned.

"Why so early?" Frank said.

"The earlier the better. You'll get to see the animals when they come to the watering holes," Fenton Hardy said. "Actually, you're lucky. Normally the park doesn't open until six, but right now the Kenyan government is very interested in making you two feel very welcome, given that you saved one of their aircraft and quite a few of their citizens. When I asked about a tour for you, they insisted on going all out."

Joe yawned. "Well, I guess I can catch up on my sleep when we get back to Bayport. This may be our only trip to Africa, so we better take advantage of every opportunity."

"True," Frank agreed reluctantly.

"That's the spirit," Fenton Hardy said.

The telephone rang the next morning at three o'clock with their wake-up call. It was accompanied by the rumbling of thunder outside their window.

Joe was surprised at how easy it was to get up. Frank had a little more trouble. But the Hardy boys made it to the lobby by four o'clock.

Their guide was already waiting for them. He recognized them immediately and introduced himself as Robert Namanga.

Robert held up a copy of a newspaper, the *Daily Nation*. There on the front page were pictures of the Hardy boys, taken at Jomo Kenyatta International Airport.

"I've been reading about you," Robert said. "You're two of the most famous people in Kenya now."

Joe took the newspaper and glanced at the article. "It takes up half the front page!" he said.

Robert nodded. "Yes. It gives a very detailed account of what happened," he said. "It also mentions why your father is here in Nairobi, and all the cases you two have solved back in Bayport. It's very interesting."

Frank got the newspaper from Joe and took a look. "Unfortunately, it may interest the wrong people," he whispered to Joe.

"I was thinking the same thing," Joe said.

"Well, are you ready to see some wild game? The Land Rover is parked outside and is running," Robert said. "If we're lucky, we'll get to see most of the park before it rains."

"We're ready!" the Hardy boys said.

At this time of morning there was almost no traffic on the streets of Nairobi, so they made good time. They left the city center and headed out on the

Mombasa Highway—it was the same route they had used the day before, coming in from the airport.

"We'll enter at the east gate. It's less traveled and has fewer roads, but that won't matter, as this vehicle can maneuver any terrain," Robert said. "We have special permission to go anywhere in the park."

They were at the east gate within twenty minutes.

"This part of the park is mostly savannah. Here's where you'll see zebra, buffalo, and antelope," Robert said. "There are also some hippos where the Mbagathi and Athi Rivers meet a little farther on."

"That's great," Joe said.

"Does the park have any big cats?" Frank asked.

Robert nodded. "You should be able to see the lions and cheetahs in the western part of the park," he said. "Rhinos, too. They're mostly in the forest glades."

"Rhinos! Now that's what I want to see!" Joe said. "Aren't they really rare?"

Robert nodded sadly. "It's a terrible situation, boys, really terrible. Poachers have almost made them extinct."

As they headed deeper into the park, sometimes using roads, sometimes not, the Hardy boys thought about the plight of the wild animals of the world. Somehow, they knew, human beings simply had to find a way to keep all of these animals alive and in their natural habitats. It would be such a tragedy if future generations were deprived of seeing them.

Three hours into the trip, the Hardy boys had seen everything that Robert Namanga had promised. Thankfully the rain had held off. The thunder and the brilliant flashes of lightning only enhanced the experience, making it even more dramatic.

When they reached the Hippo Pool, at the confluence of the Mbagathi and Athi Rivers, the skies finally opened up. The Hardys and Robert couldn't see more than a few feet in front of them.

"We'd better just stay where we are," Robert said. "The rivers and streams will soon be flooded, and I don't want to take a chance of driving into one of them to become crocodile food!"

"I'm with you on that," Joe agreed.

Frank nodded, smirking.

After a couple of hours, when the rain still hadn't let up at all, Robert said, "I'm beginning to change my mind. Let's chance it. Maybe we should try to get out while we still can."

When Robert explained that the Mbagathi and Athi might flood enough to surround them with crocodile-infested water, the Hardy boys agreed that it might be a good idea after all to see if they could get out of the park.

They had gone only a couple of miles before the Land Rover stalled and became mired in mud up to its axles. Nothing Robert could think of would free it.

"Cheetah Gate is just a few miles from here," Robert said. "Are you boys up for the walk?"

Joe took one look at the swirling water outside the Land Rover and said, "I don't think we have a choice. It doesn't take much for rushing water to move a vehicle. It won't be long until we're floating down the Mbagathi."

"Grab those ponchos in the back. They'll help keep us dry," Robert said. "I've got three bottles of water in my knapsack. That'll last us a while."

"Well, that's one thing I don't think we have to worry about," Joe joked. "If we run out, we can just hold the bottles up to the sky!"

The three of them put on the yellow ponchos, then exited the Land Rover. From where they were standing, Frank could see nothing but water. The rain was still coming down, although not as hard as before.

"Follow me," Robert said, "and if you see a floating log, it's probably a crocodile."

Frank and Joe looked at each other. They were both thinking the same thing. Whatever their friends back in Bayport were doing now, they were sure it didn't include wading in water full of crocodiles.

Fortunately Robert had a good sense of direction. Soon they were mostly out of the water, and on soggy land. He stopped for a minute to survey the area around them. Suddenly he felt his pocket. "I left my cell phone in the Land Rover!" He shook his head in disgust. "Oh, well, maybe we won't need it. The road to Cheetah Gate is mostly flooded, so we'll have to use the higher ground around it. We're south of the river, so I think we can make it to safety without having to cross any more really deep water. Some of the terrain in the Mbagathi Gorge is pretty rugged, so be careful."

"We can handle that," Joe assured him. "We stay in pretty good shape year-round."

"Coach requires quite a few hours in the weight room every week," Frank added.

For the next hour they walked in a single line, with Robert in the lead. They stopped when the rain got really heavy because they were afraid they might step off into one of the deeper ravines. The deluges only lasted for a few minutes, though, so they could continue walking safely toward Cheetah Gate.

Suddenly Robert stopped. "Quick!" he whispered. "Get down!"

They squatted behind a fringe of yellow acacia trees and looked in the direction Robert was pointing. Through the veil of light rain, they saw three men in one of the ravines. Two of the men were carrying a pole to which a cheetah had been tied by its legs. The third man was Jackson!

"Poachers. They've killed one of the cheetahs!" Robert said. "Don't they care that there are only a few left in the wild?"

"I doubt if the man in the lead cares about much of anything," Frank said.

Robert looked at him. "Do you know him?"

Joe explained their connection to Jackson. "We had a hunch he was going to do something like this," he said.

"We can't let them get away. We have to stop them," Robert said. "Are you boys up to a detour?"

"You can count on us!" Frank said.

"We'd like nothing better than to put an end to what that creep's up to," Joe added.

8 Escape!

Once they were out from behind the yellow acacia trees, Robert and the Hardy boys had no cover. But luck was with them as they made their way down the ravine—they weren't spotted and no one slipped. They finally made it to the floor, where they took cover behind the seasonal long grass.

"Those guys up ahead are not the only enemy," Robert whispered to them as they crouched behind the long grass. "Remember that the big feral cats often use this grass for cover while they stalk their prey."

"We won't forget," Joe assured him.

Slowly they started toward the three men. Now sheets of heavy rain masked their movements through the grass. As they got closer, they could hear voices—but Frank soon realized that they weren't speaking English.

"Do you understand them?" Joe whispered to Robert.

Robert nodded. "They're speaking Swahili."

"I knew I should have brought my Swahili phrase book," Frank said.

Robert grinned at him. "Well, it's not exactly tourist Swahili," he said. "Some of those words probably aren't in most dictionaries."

"What are they saying?" Frank asked.

Robert cupped his ears and tilted his head so it would be aimed in the direction of the voices. "They're saying that this cat will bring them a lot of money," he said.

Frank could tell by the sound of the voices that they were getting closer. He could hardly wait to see the expression on Jackson's face.

"What's the plan, Robert?" Frank asked.

Robert opened his safari jacket and took out a gun. "This is the only language that most poachers understand," he said. "When we get close enough, we'll try to take them by surprise. If we're lucky, they'll drop the cheetah and walk ahead of us until we reach Cheetah Gate."

Joe didn't want to admit that this plan sounded kind of weak to him. Robert was the expert in matters relating to poachers in Africa, so Joe wasn't going to suggest an alternative. Still, he knew, it would be best to be on guard for anything that could happen.

The Hardy boys and Robert were now just a few feet behind the three men. Through the tall grass the boys could see two of the men continue to chatter away in Swahili. The magnificent cheetah swung lazily back and forth on the wooden pole that the men were carrying on their shoulders.

What a waste! Frank thought. He visualized the cheetah racing through the bush after its prey. It would have been a wonderful sight to behold.

Suddenly Robert stopped. "I think it's time we take them," he whispered. "They've started to turn south, which will take them out of the park. That's probably where their cohorts are waiting for them."

"We're ready," the Hardy boys said.

"Let's go!" Robert whispered.

With Robert in the lead, his gun aimed at the men, the three of them raced through the tall grass.

When they were right behind the last man, Robert raised his pistol in the air and fired.

The two startled Africans dropped the pole with the cheetah and ran off into the bush.

Jackson turned and blinked in disbelief. He had a bloody *panga*—a large knife—in his hand. He waved it angrily at the two fleeing men and yelled something in Swahili. The men ignored him and within seconds had disappeared into the bush.

"They probably won't stop until they're in Tanzania," Robert said under his breath. He kept walking toward the man, his gun pointed straight at him.

Suddenly Jackson threw his knife toward Robert. Before Robert could react, the panga sliced into his side, causing him to drop the gun.

In seconds Jackson was almost upon them.

With one glance at each other, the Hardy boys had already decided what they had to do. Joe grabbed the panga, which had fallen to the ground, and Frank grabbed Robert's gun.

Robert now had a large rock in his hands. He shouted, "Get the cheetah! Take it to Cheetah Gate!" right before Jackson slammed into his body. Jackson fell to the ground and looked like he was out cold.

Joe grabbed one end of the pole, and Frank grabbed the other. They started running.

Adrenaline carried them the first hundred yards. When they finally looked back, they saw Robert trying to get up. When Robert saw them looking, he motioned for them to go on.

"I hate to leave him here," Frank said. "I know that panga cut him."

"He just wants to make sure the poachers don't get this cheetah," Joe said. "Even though it's dead, they won't have the satisfaction of selling the skin to some unscrupulous buyer."

The Hardy boys started up the slope of the ravine. When they reached the top, they again stopped to look down to the forest floor. Robert was moving slowly, bent over and holding his side. He had made some progress in their direction. Behind him, Jackson was still on the ground, also moving slowly.

"Change of plans," Frank said. "I say we wait for Robert."

"Yeah. It just occurred to me that once we reach the top of the ravine, I'll have no idea of where to go," Joe said.

When Robert was almost to the top of the ravine, he saw the Hardy boys waiting for him. Initially he was clearly angry, but his anger soon dissipated, and a smile appeared on his face.

"I'm beginning to believe everything I read about you in the newspaper this morning," Robert said. "You two really are special."

The Hardy boys grinned and helped Robert the rest of the way to the top.

Jackson was now standing unsteadily, looking around. He finally spotted the Hardys and Robert standing at the top of the ravine. He shook his fist angrily, and started toward them. After a few steps he fell to the ground, but he was up in seconds and making his way slowly toward them. It was almost like a scene out of a horror movie.

"We need to get started, Robert. Jackson is headed in our direction," Frank said. "He's not going to give up."

"If I had had a better angle, I could have gotten

in a harder blow with that rock," Robert said, "and that guy would have been out cold longer."

Robert insisted that he could manage to walk on his own now that he was on flatter land, so Frank and Joe gave him his gun and the panga. The three of them then headed in the direction of Cheetah Gate.

"If we keep the river in sight, we should reach Cheetah Gate in a few hours," Robert told them.

They were able to cover more distance than the Hardy boys had thought they could. Robert seemed to be able to walk faster with every few feet—but from time to time, he'd stop to rest, and would tell Frank and Joe that they should go on ahead.

They had just skirted around a fringe of yellow acacias when they literally ran into four men carrying pangas.

Frank and Joe recognized two of the men immediately. They were the ones who had been carrying the cheetah. They hadn't run away out of fear, and they were definitely not in Tanzania. They had gone to fetch some of their fellow poachers to take back the cheetah.

"Drop the pole and run, boys!" Robert cried. "Get to Cheetah Gate and send the police back!"

Without hesitating, the Hardy boys did as Robert commanded them. They knew they were no match for four men with sharp knives.

They started running through the tall grass, but one of the poachers was coming after them—with his panga raised.

Without the burden of the cheetah on the pole, the boys could run faster. The idea of leaving such a magnificent animal and Robert at the mercy of the poachers disturbed them—but if they could reach Cheetah Gate in time, they might be able to save Robert. These men knew that the Hardy boys could identify them. That might count for something.

Soon they were on a rise, and down below, Frank could see the river. It was overflowing, lapping at the edges of the road. All of a sudden they saw one of the tourist minibuses. It had stopped so some of the passengers could look at something in the water. *Crocodiles,* Frank thought.

"Joe! Look!" Frank shouted without breaking stride. "I say we head for that bus!"

Joe looked over his shoulder. The man with the panga raised was still coming after them. "Good idea," he said. He knew from watching the Summer Olympic Games on television that many Kenyans were long-distance runners, practicing daily by running across the savannah and the hills and mountains in their country. He doubted if this poacher would ever be a member of Kenya's Olympic team, but that still didn't mean that he couldn't run as fast and as far as they could.

Below them Frank could see that the tourists had begun to reboard the bus.

"Hey! Wait for us!" Frank shouted. "We need a ride to Cheetah Gate!"

One lone passenger was still taking photographs of something in the water. Joe hoped he wanted to take plenty of pictures.

Just then the bus driver honked the horn. The passenger looked up, held up one finger—probably to indicate that he had one more frame—and looked back toward the river.

Thank you! Thank you! Frank thought.

Unfortunately the passenger snapped only one more picture before boarding the bus.

"Wait! Wait!" Joe shouted. "You can't leave!"

The man with the panga was gaining on them, but seemed to be moving more cautiously now. Frank was sure he was thinking that if he could get rid of the Hardys without getting too close to the passengers on the bus, there would be no one who could identify him to the Kenyan authorities. What the poacher didn't realize, though, was that the Hardy boys could run extremely fast.

The road into the park was flooded by the river, and the driver of the bus was trying to find some dry-enough ground to turn around on. The Hardy boys thought they might make it to the road in time to catch the bus after all.

With a tremendous burst of speed, they covered

the last part of the distance between them and the bus in record time.

"I wish Coach could see us now," Joe shouted to Frank.

"I wish I had a stopwatch," Frank said. "I think we just broke a world record."

By the time the Hardys got to the road, the bus driver had succeeded in turning around, and was just starting to gain some speed. He had to slam on the brakes to keep from hitting the boys.

Frank and Joe started banging on the door, startling both the driver and the passengers. For a minute it looked like the driver wasn't going to open the door, but he did finally. As they climbed aboard, Joe looked through one of the bus windows. He saw the poacher standing on the rise the boys had just come from, about a hundred yards away. Joe could only wonder what was going through the poacher's mind.

"What's the meaning of this?" the driver was demanding of Frank. "You can't pick up one of these buses on a whim."

Frank quickly explained that they needed to contact the police at Cheetah Gate because poachers had killed one of the cheetahs and were holding their driver hostage.

That was all the explanation the driver needed. "Take a seat," he said. "I'll radio this information ahead to Cheetah Gate and then get us there as fast as possible."

Frank and Joe headed for two empty seats at the back of the bus and sank into the plush seats. The passengers were giving them friendly—but puzzled—looks.

"What do you think the poachers will do to Robert?" Joe whispered. "You don't think they'll kill him?"

"It could happen, Joe," Frank said. "He can identify them."

"So can we, Frank," Joe said. "And Jackson knows where to find us."

9 A Death in the Hospital

By the time the tourist minibus arrived at Cheetah Gate, the Kenya National Police helicopter had located Robert Namanga and rescued him. He was in a very bad state, having been severely beaten, but he was still able to talk.

"He's been taken to Nairobi Hospital, on Argwings Kodhek Road," Frank and Joe were told. "From what the pilot could tell, you two young men saved his life."

"How?" Joe asked.

"Well, evidently the poacher who was chasing you ran back to tell his accomplices what had happened," the guard said. "They knew the bus driver would radio Cheetah Gate and that a police helicopter would be dispatched shortly. They stopped beating Namanga and fled into the bush."

"Robert must have known what he was doing when he told us to run," Frank whispered to Joe.

Joe nodded. "Now I don't feel so bad about leaving him. If we hadn't, then none of us would be alive."

Frank and Joe rode the tourist minibus back into Nairobi. Several passengers in the tour were also staying at the New Stanley Hotel.

When the boys got to their room, Mr. Hardy was there. He was talking on the telephone to Mrs. Hardy. The boys took turns saying hello, gave brief—and censored—versions of their trip so far, then returned the phone to their father.

When Mr. Hardy finally hung up, Frank told him all about their day. "Jackson has to be stopped, Dad! Now Joe and I can prove that he trades illegal wild animal skins and other parts."

Mr. Hardy shook his head in dismay. "I talked to several policemen at the conference today," he said. "Poaching is a big problem all over the continent."

"We can give the Kenyan police a description of Jackson, Dad," Joe suggested. "That should make it easy for them to find him."

"Perhaps," Fenton Hardy said. "But from what I'm hearing, not everyone in the country thinks what the poachers are doing is bad."

The Hardy boys looked surprised.

"What do you mean, Dad?" Frank asked.

"Look at our own country, boys. It was once covered with wild game, too, but now there's very little," Mr. Hardy said. "When people move in, they expect to have land to build houses on and to farm. They don't want to coexist with wild animals."

"The difference now is that hunting protected wild animals is illegal," Frank countered. "Back then, it wasn't. We've learned a lot about how important it is for people to save the environment, and wild animals are part of the environment."

After a brief pause, Mr. Hardy nodded. "I agree," he said. "I'll set up a meeting tomorrow with Ian Malindi at Government House." He sniffed the air. "But right now I think you two need a shower to wash off some of the Nairobi National Park," he added with a grin.

Frank and Joe *completely* agreed with that.

The next morning Mr. Hardy called Dr. Malindi. He agreed to meet the Hardys for lunch to talk about the poaching incident the boys had witnessed the day before.

Mr. Hardy had his breakfast sent up to the room so he could put the finishing touches on his morning speech.

Frank and Joe took their time getting out of bed.

After Mr. Hardy had left for the conference, the Hardy boys got up, dressed, had breakfast in the Thorn Tree Café, and then roamed around the hotel, watching the guests coming and going and absorbing the excitement of Nairobi.

"I'm sore," Joe groaned.

"Me, too," Frank agreed. "What happened to a restful vacation?"

Mr. Hardy arrived back at the hotel just before noon. "The midmorning session ran a little late. It seems the news of your adventure yesterday has made the Nairobi newspapers," he explained. "We had quite a lively discussion about the future of wild animals in Africa. I'll fill you in on the way to lunch."

A black limousine met the Hardys in front of the hotel and drove them to the Ministry of the Interior at Government House. On the way, Mr. Hardy told his sons about some of the issues that were raised earlier that morning.

When the Hardys reached the ministry, they found that Dr. Malindi was waiting for them in his outer office.

"Welcome, Fenton," Dr. Malindi said. "It's so good to see you again."

"It's good to see you, too, Ian," Mr. Hardy said. "Let me introduce my sons, Frank and Joe."

Dr. Malindi shook hands with the Hardy boys. "I

feel as though I know you," he said. "You've only been here a couple of days, and already I can't turn on the television or pick up a newspaper without seeing your faces."

Frank and Joe found themselves blushing.

"The people of Kenya thank you," Dr. Malindi said.

"Well, we were just in the right place at the right time," Frank said.

"Twice," Joe said.

"I think you're being too modest," Dr. Malindi said. "Come." He motioned for them to follow him into his office. "I've had a light lunch sent in for us. I hope you'll enjoy it."

The four of them sat on comfortable couches in the corner of the large office, and dove into the meal of cold meats, cheeses, and fruit.

"I've read the accounts in the newspapers about the poaching incident, but I always like to hear things firsthand, if I can," Dr. Malindi said. "If you wouldn't mind telling me your version of the story, I'd appreciate it."

Joe recounted the events that had taken place from the time they met Robert Namanga in front of the New Stanley Hotel until the time they returned in the tourist minibus. Occasionally Frank would supply a detail that Joe had forgotten.

When the Hardy boys finished, Dr. Malindi said,

"We've known for some time that someone outside Kenya was directing the major poaching operations, but this is the first time we've been able to get this full a description of a suspect."

"We'd be willing to testify in court against him," Joe said.

Frank nodded his agreement.

"I'll remember that, boys, but unfortunately we're a long way from a courtroom appearance," Dr. Malindi said sadly.

"Why?" Frank asked. "We saw him with that cheetah."

Dr. Malindi took a deep breath. "Your father told me that you stumbled into the middle of one of our demonstrations between the farmers and the animal rights people," he said.

"We did," Joe said. "It was . . . well . . . interesting."

Dr. Malindi gave them a wan smile. "I can imagine," he said. "So you can see what we're up against. Both sides have good arguments. Our government is just trying to find a good solution to the problem, one that will please everyone.

"The poaching stops from time to time, such as when Richard Leakey was in charge of the Kenyan Wildlife Service. But then various groups in the country think things are too strict, and that they should be allowed to keep some of their old ways—so government people are sacked, and then things go back to the way they were. That is, until somebody comes along again who can put a stop to the illegal hunting once and for all."

The Hardy boys looked at each other.

"We'd like to help," Joe said.

"We'll do anything we can to stop the killing of wild animals," Frank said.

Dr. Malindi smiled at them. "Perhaps fate brought you two here. You might just be what this country needs to solve the current crisis." Dr. Malindi looked at his watch. "Fenton, I'm sorry, but there's another—"

Just then Dr. Malindi's secretary burst into the room. "I'm sorry, Mr. Minister, but Nairobi Hospital just called. There's been an incident." She looked at the Hardys, unsure if she should continue.

"It's all right," Dr. Malindi said. "Tell us what happened."

"Someone went into Robert Namanga's room and turned off all of the life-support machines," the secretary said. "I'm afraid he's . . ."

Frank and Joe looked at each other. They knew this wasn't an accident. Somebody had deliberately made sure that Robert wouldn't be able to identify the men who had beaten him.

"This isn't just a case of poaching anymore, is it, Dr. Malindi?" Frank said. "This is a case of murder."

Dr. Malindi nodded. "Nothing is sacred to these people."

Joe stood up. He was almost unable to contain his anger. After all that had happened yesterday, after they had reached the tourist minibus in time for the driver to radio Cheetah Gate, after the police helicopter had rescued Robert and taken him to the hospital—just in time to save his life—someone had slipped into the hospital and ended everything with a flick of a switch.

Dr. Malindi stood up. "I'm going to arrange for around-the-clock protection for Frank and Joe," he said to Mr. Hardy. "My people will get a description of this man Jackson. I assure you of this: If one of the poachers would do this to Robert Namanga, they wouldn't hesitate to do this to your sons." He turned to Frank and Joe. "I know that being protected will mean that you won't have as much freedom of movement for the remainder of your stay, but I think everyone in the Kenyan government would agree with me that your lives are in danger. We shouldn't take any chances."

The Hardy boys glanced at their father, to see his reaction to Dr. Malindi's pronouncement. It was exactly what they had hoped it would be. Fenton Hardy would never expect his sons to stay in a hotel room when there was detective work to be done.

As the Hardy boys followed their father and Dr. Malindi to the police car that had been summoned to take them back to the New Stanley Hotel, Frank and Joe were already plotting their next move.

10 Disguised

It wasn't easy getting out of the hotel. Dr. Malindi had been serious about police protection for the Hardy boys. There were men and women stationed at every exit and even patrolling the interior of the hotel itself.

"With our pictures in the newspapers on a daily basis, everybody in Nairobi knows what we look like. It's going to be hard slipping past any of the guards," Frank complained. "But we have to check out Mombasa Curios again. I have a hunch that the shop holds the key to this."

"I agree, Frank. We have to be creative if we're going to get out of this hotel," Joe said.

It didn't take them long to think of a way out.

One trip to the gift shop in the lobby, ostensibly

to buy some African clothing for friends, allowed them to come away with two *vikoi*—loose-fitting saronglike wraps with hoods, which were worn by both men and women.

Back in their room, the Hardy boys plotted their strategy.

"We'll take the elevator up to the fifth floor, where the swimming pool is, talking louder than we need to about how relaxing a few laps will be," Joe said. "Then, after we get up there, we'll change into the vikoi, and look for the nearest exit."

Frank agreed that it was probably the most feasible plan of action.

Joe put the vikoi in a duffel bag that looked like something people would take with them to a pool, and he and Frank left the room. They nodded to a couple of police officers who just happened to pass them in the corridor.

The police officers stopped, waited to see which button the Hardy boys pushed on the elevator, and, when Joe pushed the up arrow, continued on down the corridor.

"That was easy," Joe whispered.

"Don't jinx it," Frank said. "We haven't gotten to the hard part yet."

When they reached the fifth floor, the elevator doors opened to a waiting police officer—giving both boys a momentary shock.

"We were thinking about going for a swim," Frank managed to say.

He didn't want to lie to the man. They actually *had* been thinking about swimming—earlier that morning.

The police officer smiled. "It's a nice pool," he said.

As the boys stepped out of the elevator, the policeman stepped into it.

"For a minute there," Joe said, "I thought he was going to call our bluff."

"Well, let's not wait around to see if he changes his mind," Frank said. "Let's get this show on the road."

Frank and Joe were glad that no one else in the New Stanley Hotel had decided to take a swim. They were alone in the pool area. They made a complete circle of the deck, looking for the right exit, and finally decided that the best idea would be for them to dress in the vikoi, take the stairs down one floor, and then take the elevator back down to the ground floor.

"They won't be expecting that," Frank said.

They hurriedly put the vikoi on over their regular clothes and set the empty duffel bag on top of one of the lockers. Mr. Hardy's name was on a tag attached to the handle, so whoever found it would know who it belonged to and would surely return it to their room.

Disguised, the Hardy boys quickly made their

way to their chosen exit, opened the door slowly, and peered into the stairwell. No one was in sight. Frank and Joe slipped through the door and headed to the fourth floor. When they got to the fire door, Joe opened it slowly and looked out. Two police officers were in the corridor, walking the other way.

"Well, it'll either work or it won't, Frank," Joe whispered. "Let's see what happens."

The Hardy boys slipped into the corridor as quickly and as quietly as they could. They didn't want the two police officers to turn around and see them coming from the stairwell. If they turned around, the boys hoped the police officers would just think they were coming from one of the rooms on this floor.

Frank and Joe made their way to the elevator without being noticed.

Joe pushed the down arrow.

By then the police officers had turned a corner in the rambling corridor that would take them into another wing.

"So far, so good," Frank whispered.

"I just hope that the lobby is crowded as usual," Joe whispered back. "Maybe there will be other men dressed the way we are."

Luck was with them. Nobody paid any attention to the two men dressed in vikoi who made their way through the crowd toward the exit onto Kimathi Street.

Outside, they turned left, which took them to Kenyatta Avenue, then right for two more blocks, until they were on Moi Avenue.

Joe looked at his reflection in some of the shop windows they passed. "I don't recognize myself," he said to Frank.

"Let's hope the man in the curio shop won't recognize us from the other day, either," Frank said.

When they reached the front of Mombasa Curios, they pretended to look at the wares in the window.

"Do you see anyone we know inside?" Joe whispered.

"It's hard to tell. The shop is too dark, and what I'm mostly seeing is the reflection of the passing cars," Frank said. "We'll have to take a chance and go inside."

"If we keep our faces away from the shopkeeper as much as possible, maybe we can find out what we need to know without being exposed," Joe said.

"On three, then," Frank said. He counted to three, took a breath, and opened the shop door.

The bell jangled.

"May I help you?" a woman's voice asked.

Frank tried to disguise his voice. "We just want to look, thank you," he said. "We're not sure what we want to buy."

The woman went back to reading a magazine.

Frank and Joe made their way slowly through the shop. From time to time they'd pick up a carving, examine it, then replace it.

They were at the rear of the shop when the bell on the front door jangled again. Two elderly American couples had entered, talking rather loudly about what they had seen in the previous shop.

"They were much too expensive," one of the men said. "Let's see what this place charges for the same thing."

The woman at the counter had laid down her magazine and was approaching the couples with a smile. She had a hard time keeping up with them, because they were moving quickly through the store.

"Oh, these prices are wonderful," one woman said. "I can get twice as much here as I could in that other shop."

"Yes, and the quality is just as good, too," the other woman said. "Why do you think he charged so much?" She turned to the woman who was showing one of the men a mask. "Why does that shop two doors down charge so much? It's outrageous. Your things are just as good—probably better."

The woman gave her a weak smile.

"What do you call those?"

Frank turned to see one of the men looking at him.

"Excuse me?" Frank said, trying to maintain

the accent he had used with the shopkeeper.

"That hooded robe thing you have on," the man repeated. "What do you call that?"

"It's called a—," Frank started to say.

But one of the women said, "Dear! Dear! Come here! You're not going to believe this! Don't you think Bob and JoAnn would just love to have one of these in their den?"

The man didn't wait for Frank to finish the answer to his question before he departed to see what his wife was looking at.

"Good. That was close. Maybe they'll be occupied for a while," Frank whispered to Joe. He nodded to the door that led to the back of the shop. "It's not closed. Did you notice that?"

Joe nodded. "Let's get close while we can. Maybe we can overhear something."

At that moment the bell on the door jangled again. This time it wasn't tourists looking for gifts to take back home with them. It was Jackson.

Frank and Joe ducked behind one of the shelves.

Without looking at anything or anyone, Jackson barged into the storeroom. He closed the door, but left it slightly ajar.

Immediately Frank and Joe hurried to the door to listen.

"He just called me from New York," Jackson said.

"Why did he call you? I'm the one in charge of

his business operations in Kenya. And *you* report to *me*." Frank and Joe recognized the voice. It was the shopkeeper they had talked to on their previous visit.

"He said your line was busy," Jackson explained. "He wanted to tell us that he's not happy about what happened in the park yesterday."

"Why would he be?" the shopkeeper said. "That cheetah's skin lost a lot of value because of your carelessness. You can't drag them or drop them and expect people to pay top prices."

"It's those Hardy boys," Jackson said. "He blames them for trying to destroy his business."

"He needs to forget about those boys and take care of what's really important," the shopkeeper said.

"Such as?" Jackson said.

"The black rhino!" the shopkeeper said. "My men have located one for him."

"A black rhino! That's perfect," Jackson said. "He's always wanted a black rhino. He'll pay a fortune for it! That'll make up for our other losses."

"I know," the shopkeeper said. "We can arrange for him to kill it in the wild himself."

"How?" Jackson asked.

"It's all in knowing the right people," the shopkeeper told him.

"Well, maybe he can take care of two things at once," Jackson said.

"What do you mean?" the shopkeeper asked.

"When he comes from New York in two days," Jackson said, "he can kill both the Hardy boys *and* the black rhino."

11 The Secret of the Hotel Zebra

The Hardy boys were barely able to hide before the door to the stockroom flung open and Jackson rushed out.

"Come on, Frank! We have to follow him," Joe whispered. "If we find out where he's staying, we can inform the police, and maybe they'll take him in for questioning."

Frank hesitated. "You're not forgetting that he wants to kill us, are you?" he whispered.

Joe shook his head.

The Hardy boys started for the front door of the shop.

"Hey, you never did tell me what you call that thing you're wearing," the American tourist called to them.

"Vikoi," Frank called back without looking at the man.

"What?" the man asked.

But Frank and Joe were already out the door and hurrying down Moi Avenue, trying to keep up with Jackson.

"I hope where he's going isn't too far from here," Frank said. "I don't want to chase him all over Nairobi!"

As Jackson neared the corner of Moi Avenue and Biashara Street, he began to slow his pace. Finally he halted in front of a bus stop.

The Hardy boys stopped near a shop two doors down.

"Do you have any money for a bus ride, Joe?" Frank asked.

Joe nodded.

Just then a Kenya Bus Service vehicle pulled up to the stop. Frank noticed that the sign on the front indicated that it went to River Road.

"I read about that area. It's not the best part of Nairobi," Frank said. "What do you think we should do?"

"We don't have a choice, Frank," Joe said. "This guy is doing some serious damage."

"You're right," Frank said as Jackson stepped onto the bus. "Come on!"

The Hardys ran toward the bus. Just as the doors

began to close, they jumped on and took seats at the back.

Jackson was sitting two seats behind the driver. He hadn't even looked up when the Hardy boys passed him. Joe thought that his mind was probably still on the conversation he had just had with the shopkeeper in Mombasa Curios.

As the bus lumbered along River Road, Frank tried to memorize some of the landmarks. He knew that bus service in Nairobi was almost nonexistent at night, and that if they had trouble finding a taxi, they might have to walk back to the New Stanley Hotel.

As the bus was nearing Munyu Road, Jackson pulled the cord—to signal the driver that he wanted to get off—and started walking toward the front of the bus. Frank and Joe stood up, too, but stayed where they were on the bus until Jackson was on the sidewalk. The boys then discreetly followed the man off the bus.

Jackson started walking down Munyu Road.

The Hardy boys followed at a safe distance. The area they were in was full of seedy hotels, night clubs, and secondhand clothing stores. Frank and Joe initially felt out of place, but they soon realized that with the vikoi, they fit right in. Nobody was paying any attention to them.

"I'm glad you thought of buying these clothes, Joe," Frank whispered. "These are perfect disguises."

Two blocks from River Road Jackson entered the Hotel Zebra. The front of the building was painted with black and white stripes. The Hardys could hear loud music coming from somewhere on the first floor.

"We've got to follow him inside," Joe said. "We have to find out what room he's staying in."

"Well, we've fooled everyone so far. Nobody has looked at us like we're two American boys from Bayport," Frank said. "Maybe our luck will hold in the Hotel Zebra."

With that, Frank and Joe entered the hotel. They immediately found themselves in a crowd of people who seemed to be using the lobby for a party.

The Hardy boys made their way slowly through the mass of people toward the rear of the lobby. There they caught sight of Jackson heading up some stairs.

"Come on, Frank! I don't think there's too much security in this place," Joe whispered. "I doubt if anybody will try to stop us from following him."

By the time the Hardy boys reached the bottom of the steps, Jackson was already on the second landing.

Frank grabbed Joe by the arm. "Maybe he's leading us into a trap," he whispered. "This seems too easy."

Joe considered that. "We have to take the chance,

Frank. He's looking for two teenage American boys in jeans and sneakers. He's not looking for two Kenyans dressed in vikoi."

"True," Frank said.

They quickened their pace up the stairs. When they reached the second landing, they heard Jackson above them—so they headed up to the third floor.

Frank had noticed that the Hotel Zebra had four stories. Jackson stopped on the third floor and headed down the dimly lit hallway.

"This is definitely not a four-star hotel," Joe whispered.

"You got that right," Frank agreed.

Just as they were passing a door, it opened, and a man came out. He was draped in a towel, and he was heading down the hallway.

"A communal bathroom," Joe observed. He suddenly had an idea.

Up ahead Jackson was unlocking a door. After struggling with the lock for several seconds, the door finally opened and Jackson went inside.

"Quick!" Frank said. "Let's find out the number."

They hurried along the corridor until they reached the room Jackson had entered.

"Room Thirty-seven," Frank said. "That's the information we'll give the police. Come on."

"We may be able to give the police some other information, Frank, if we just wait long enough,"

Joe said. He motioned toward the far end of the corridor, which was even dimmer than where they were standing. "Let's wait for a few minutes."

"Why, Joe?" Frank asked. "We have what we came for."

"That communal bathroom gave me an idea," Joe said. "If Jackson takes a bath, then we can search his room. We might be able to find the name of this man who's coming in two days."

"You're right. There may be a telephone number or something," Frank said. "But what makes you think he's going to take a bath?"

Joe shrugged. "He looks like an American, and most Americans are used to washing themselves daily," he explained.

"Won't he take the key to the room with him?" Frank said.

"He had trouble opening the door, so I think he'll take a chance," Joe said. "I doubt if he keeps anything he considers valuable in the room, anyway."

After an hour of waiting Joe was about to concede that he had been wrong. But just then Jackson's door opened, and he exited, wearing only a towel. He headed down the hall toward the communal bathroom. And he hadn't locked the door!

Once Jackson was inside, Joe said, "Let's do it!"

Frank and Joe hurried down the hall and quickly went inside Jackson's room.

It was as seedy as the rest of the hotel. There was a small chest against one wall, with a couple of the drawers pulled out halfway. A suitcase was lying open at the foot of the chest. The boys couldn't tell if Jackson had been packing or unpacking. There was an unmade double bed on the far side of the room. The open window just above it was letting in plenty of noise from the street below. Outside the window, the Hardy boys could see the frame of a rickety old metal fire escape.

"That's comforting," Joe said with a hint of sarcasm in his voice. "This place is a real firetrap!"

"Let's start looking," Frank said. "Jackson doesn't strike me as the kind who spends much time soaking."

Frank started with the suitcase.

"I'll search his wallet," Joe said.

He picked up Jackson's wallet off the top of the chest, flipped it open, and looked in the bill section. When he found nothing except some American and Kenyan currency, he looked through the other pockets. Just as he was about to put it back on the chest, he stopped. "Hey, Frank! Take a look," he said. "There's something weird here."

Frank stopped his search of Jackson's suitcase and looked at what Joe was pointing to.

"It's his driver's license," Frank said. "He's just as ugly as his picture."

"Look at the name," Joe said.

Frank looked closely at the tiny print. "Harry Andrews," he read. The address was in Long Island City. Frank looked up at Joe. "I thought Mr. Watson said his name was Jackson."

"He did," Joe said.

"Well, maybe that's what Andrews told him," Frank said. "He probably has plenty of aliases."

"That's probably it," Joe agreed.

Just then, they heard voices out in the hall. One of them belonged to the man they had been calling Jackson. At that moment, the door to the room began to open.

There was no time to make it out the window.

"Quick!" Frank whispered. "Under the bed!"

The Hardys dove under the bed just as Andrews entered the room.

He spent several minutes cursing whoever it was had stopped him in the hall for money. Clearly, there was no way that he was going to give away any of his hard-earned cash.

The Hardy boys were finding it hard to keep from sneezing because of the thick dust on the floor, but Joe's sniffling was overpowered by the angry words from Andrews.

"I hope he's planning to go out for the evening," Frank whispered. "I don't think I can stay down here much longer."

Andrews yawned, muttered something unintelligible, turned out the light, and headed toward the bed.

"Uh-oh!" Joe whispered to Frank.

They weren't prepared for how low the bed sank when Andrews fell onto it.

Frank and Joe both let out small groans.

Andrews jumped up. "What the . . ." He tripped over the suitcase and crashed to the floor. This was followed by a string of curse words in several languages.

Frank and Joe jumped out from under the bed. They had to get out of the room, but Andrews was between them and the door—and they could just make out his outline as he began to lift himself off the floor.

"The fire escape!" Frank whispered. "It's the only way out!"

At that moment Andrews lunged across the bed. He barely missed them as Frank and Joe tumbled out the window onto the landing of the metal fire escape.

The Hardy boys started down the escape, but part of the frame had detached itself from the side of the building. They had to hold on tightly to the rail as they ran down the steps to the next landing.

Andrews was obviously used to getting dressed in a hurry, because by the time the Hardy boys had reached the bottom of the fire escape, Andrews, fully clothed, was already on his way down.

Frank and Joe jumped down from the escape and landed in the alley together. They immediately headed toward Munyu Road.

The crowds were thicker along the street now. The clubs were really lively.

"Let's head for River Road," Frank said. "Maybe we'll luck out and find either a bus or a taxi that'll take us back to the city center."

The Hardy boys didn't want to run, because they were sure it would attract attention and probably give the street crowds the impression that they were up to trouble. But one look over their shoulders let them know that Andrews had reached the end of the alley, and was running up the street after them. They had to hurry.

Frank and Joe began walking as fast as they could, weaving in and out of the crowds of people on the sidewalk. Finally they reached River Road.

Frank ran up to a man standing on the corner. "Is there a bus or a taxi we could take back to the New Stanley Hotel?"

The man laughed. "No bus. No taxi," he said.

Joe glanced around and looked back down Munyu Road. Harry Andrews was closing in.

12 Under Surveillance

Right up River Road, about a half block away, a taxi pulled up to the curb in front of a busy nightclub. Two young couples got out. One of the men handed the driver what looked like a lot of money. "Be back in two hours," he said. He spoke loudly, with an English accent. "And I'll double that."

"Yes, sir!" the driver said.

"Taxi! Taxi!" Joe shouted. "Wait!"

He and Frank tore up the crowded sidewalk as fast as they could. The two couples stared at them in shock.

"We need to get to the New Stanley Hotel as quickly as possible!" Frank shouted to the driver.

Behind them, Harry Andrews had turned the corner and was racing toward them.

"Well, get in," the driver said. "That'll be something for me to do while I wait to pick up these rich people!"

The Hardy boys jumped into the taxi. It pulled out into traffic just before Harry Andrews reached them.

"Man, that was close," Joe whispered.

They looked out the rear window to see Andrews scowling at them.

"Do you think he recognized us?" Joe said.

"If he shows up at the hotel tonight, then I guess he did," Frank replied.

"And if he doesn't show up?" Joe said.

"Well, in that case, he'll probably let the man who's coming in two days 'take care of us,'" Frank said.

Joe shivered. "I don't really like either choice," he said.

"Me, either," Frank agreed.

"We need to let the police . . . ," Joe started to say. It suddenly occurred to them both that by now the police stationed in the hotel knew they weren't on the fifth floor swimming.

"We're going to have a lot of explaining to do," Joe finished.

When they reached the hotel, Joe had just enough money to pay the taxi driver the fare and give him a meager tip.

The Hardy boys had barely entered the lobby when they were met by Mr. Hardy and Dr. Malindi.

"Are you boys hungry?" Mr. Hardy asked them.

Dr. Malindi gave him a surprised look. This was obviously not the question he would have asked his sons if they had been missing for several hours after having given a large percentage of the Nairobi police department the slip.

Frank and Joe nodded.

"How did you guess?" Joe asked.

"Good. I have a reservation for a table for four in the Tate Room," Mr. Hardy said, naming the New Stanley's main restaurant. "We can eat, and then you can fill Dr. Malindi and me in on what's been happening to you since you left the hotel." Mr. Hardy winked at his sons.

Most of the restaurant's guests had already ordered and were in the midst of enjoying dinner, so it didn't take the Hardys and Dr. Malindi long to be served.

Frank and Joe told Fenton Hardy and Dr. Malindi everything that had happened to them, from the information about the man who was coming from the United States in two days to kill both the black rhino and the Hardy boys, to the race with Harry Andrews down River Road.

By dessert Dr. Malindi was convinced that the boys knew what they were doing.

"Harry Andrews lives in Long Island City, New York. That's what his driver's license says," Joe said. "He must have given Mr. Watson a fake name, because Mr. Watson called him Jackson."

"That could be one of his aliases," Dr. Malindi suggested.

"That's what we thought, too," Frank said.

Dr. Malindi had written everything down. Now he picked up his cell phone and dialed a number. He gave the information to the person on the other end of the line.

"Are the police going to pick up Andrews tonight?" Joe asked.

Dr. Malindi shook his head. "We can wait two more days for him, if it means we might get all of these culprits. We certainly don't want to take a chance on tipping off the mastermind behind all of this," he said. "I've sent some men to the River Road area to keep an eye on Harry Andrews. They won't lose him."

As they left the restaurant, Dr. Malindi told the boys that he had arranged for them to take guided tours of several of the important museums, art galleries, and other points of interest in Nairobi.

Frank and Joe accepted this gesture, even though they knew that the invitation had been offered so that the Kenyan authorities could keep an eye on them.

"We'll probably get enough information for a dozen term papers," Frank said, "so this won't be too bad."

Joe didn't even want to think about school.

As it turned out, the next day was one of the highlights of the trip.

The Railway Museum particularly interested Joe. Outside there was a collection of old locomotives and carriages, most of them built in England. Some of the moving stock had been used in the filming of movies set in Nairobi.

Frank thought the National Museum was the best. He stayed for a long time in the Prehistory Gallery, where there were reproductions of Tanzanian rock paintings and casts of wide-splayed, human-looking footprints—a small pair following a larger pair, which were discovered at Laetoli, in Tanzania. A guide told them that the footprints almost certainly belonged to *Homo erectus*, who many people thought were the direct ancestors of modern human beings.

The Hardy boys were surprised when Dr. Malindi called them early on the morning of the second day of touring to ask them if they would like to accompany him to Jomo Kenyatta International Airport to meet the arriving flights with Americans on the passenger manifest. His plan, he explained, was to look for anyone suspicious.

Frank and Joe quickly agreed.

Once they were at the airport, they went immediately to the international arrivals area. A uniformed man handed Dr. Malindi a stack of papers.

"These are the flight manifests," Dr. Malindi told them. "Today there are fifteen Americans arriving in Kenya. Thank goodness it's a slow day."

"Where are they coming from?" Joe asked.

"Well, let's see," Dr. Malindi began. "There are five arriving on a Kenya International Airways flight from New York. There are two arriving on Air France from Paris, three arriving on British Airways from London, one arriving on Olympic from Athens, one arriving on EgyptAir from Cairo, and three arriving on El Al from Tel Aviv."

"How many of these passengers are men?" Frank asked.

"Twelve," Dr. Malindi said.

"I think the Kenya International Airways flight is our best bet," Joe said. "Why would he want to go through Europe?"

"Well, for one thing, the flight from New York is very long, and some people just don't like to fly that many hours at once," Frank said. "Flying through Europe breaks up the flight, and it usually costs about the same amount of money as a direct flight."

Dr. Malindi nodded.

"We're going to have people meeting all of the flights, looking for men who fit a certain profile," Dr. Malindi said, "but I think you and I should stay by the flights arriving from New York and London. I have a gut feeling that our man will be on one of those."

Unfortunately, at the end of the day, no one who disembarked even remotely fit the profile the Nairobi police were working from.

Six of the men were businessmen who were met by Kenyan representatives of their companies. Five of the men were college students from Texas Tech University. They were on their way to a biological research project in southern Kenya.

The remaining man introduced himself to the Hardys and Dr. Malindi as a retired professor of African languages. Dr. G. Cranston Douglas had come to Kenya to write a linguistics paper comparing the names of certain types of fish in the coastal Bantu languages of Swahili, Mijikenda, Segeju, Pokomo, Taita, and Taveta. He looked like a character out of an old *Tarzan* movie. He was wearing a safari jacket and had a sweat-stained pith helmet on his head. He needed a cane to help him walk. The head of the cane was the carved face of a baboon.

Dr. Douglas made his way to the stop for the shuttle to the New Stanley Hotel, only to find that the bus had broken down. Dr. Malindi offered to drop him off at the hotel when he dropped off the Hardy boys. The professor readily accepted.

Although Frank and Joe couldn't be sure, it seemed to them that some of the authorities were less than friendly as their group made its way through the airport to Dr. Malindi's car. Even Dr. Malindi didn't have much to say on the drive back into Nairobi, although the boys thought that might have something to do with their guest, Dr. Douglas.

When they arrived at the hotel, Frank pulled Dr. Douglas's luggage out of Dr. Malindi's car and gave it to a porter. Dr. Douglas thanked them for the ride and went into the hotel to register.

Just as the Hardy boys started toward the hotel's entrance, Dr. Malindi stopped them. "I don't know what to think, boys. I really don't," he said. "We'll keep watching Mr. Andrews for a few more days, to see if anything happens—but I'm starting to wonder if your information wasn't right. You'll only be here for a few more days. Perhaps you'd better just forget about the detective work for a while and enjoy the sights of Kenya?"

He gave them a smile and drove away.

The Hardy boys looked at each other.

"You know what?" Joe said. "I think we've just been told to mind our own business—in a very diplomatic way."

"No kidding," Frank agreed.

"There's no way I can give up now, though," Joe said.

"I'm with you," Frank said. "We're not going to let anyone kill a black rhino—or anything else!"

13 Fire!

When the Hardy boys got to their room, they found a note from their father. He wrote that he had been invited to spend a couple of days at Mfangano Island Camp in Lake Victoria with some of the other conference participants.

"Dad has all the luck. We actually just learned about Lake Victoria in geography a couple of weeks ago," Frank said. "I'd love to go there."

He told Joe what he remembered from class. Lake Victoria was the second largest fresh water lake in the world. Little was known about it outside of Africa until the nineteenth century, when European explorers declared it as the source of the Nile. Three countries border the lake—Kenya, Uganda, and Tanzania.

Joe was reading through a guide book that had been on their father's bedside table. "It looks like the only way to get to the island is to take a single-engine plane from Masai Mara, fly over the escarpment to Mfangano Island, and then take one of the camp's motorboats around the island to the bay that shelters Mfangano Island Camp." Joe closed the book and put it back on the table. "Sounds cool."

Frank yawned. "What do you want to do? It's too early to go to bed."

Joe yawned, too. "You know, I'd kind of like to see a movie. An American one," Joe said. "I can't believe it, but I'm feeling sort of homesick. If we were in Bayport right now, we could go to one of the multiplex theaters."

"They're called cinemas here. Kenya mostly imports American and Indian films," Frank said. He looked around the room and found a copy of the *Daily Nation* lying on the floor next to his father's bed. He checked the index and found the page that advertised the movies that were showing. "Joe—look!" he said. "This could be Bayport."

Joe came over to where Frank was sitting on the floor and plopped down beside him. "Hey, that's one I missed. I thought I'd have to wait until it came out on video. Who thought I'd have a chance to see it in Kenya?"

Frank looked at the address of the theater. "That's kind of far from here—in one of the western suburbs,

I think," he said. "I don't think we should go too far tonight."

They scanned the rest of the listings, lingering from time to time on some of the Indian films with really interesting titles. They finally decided to go to a movie they had already seen, because it was at a theater on Kenyatta Avenue—just a block from the New Stanley Hotel.

On their way out, the boys saw Dr. Douglas and said hello to him.

"Did you get settled in?" Frank asked.

Dr. Douglas nodded. "Yes. This is a very nice hotel. I'm glad I decided to stay here. Are you two headed out for a night on the town?"

"We're going to see a movie," Joe replied. "It's showing just down the street."

"Well, that's a nice way to spend a few hours," Dr. Douglas said. "I hope you enjoy it."

"Thanks," the Hardy boys said.

"Have a good night," Frank added.

"Oh, I shall, I shall," Dr. Douglas assured them.

The Hardy boys knew when they left the lobby that they'd have a police escort, but they didn't care. The officer might like the movie they were taking him to.

The theater was crowded, and Frank and Joe had to sit closer to the front of the auditorium than they preferred. There were times when Frank and Joe were the only ones in the theater laughing about what the characters were doing. Frank soon realized that the humor would probably only make sense to an American.

When the movie was over, Frank and Joe filed out with the rest of the crowd. They reached the lobby and Joe wondered what would happen if Harry Andrews had decided to see this movie, too. It wasn't long until they spotted their police escort, who, instead of seeing the movie, had apparently just waited outside the theater for them.

Once they were back at the hotel, the boys lingered in the gift shop for a few minutes and talked about getting something to eat at the Thorn Tree Café. They decided just to go to bed; it had been a long day.

Frank woke up with a start. The room was full of thick smoke. He could hardly breathe.

"Joe!" he managed to shout. "We have to get out of here!"

When his brother didn't answer him, Frank rushed to Joe's side, shook him, and, when that didn't work, rolled him out of bed and onto the floor.

Finally Joe came to life—but he started wheezing. He was clearly having difficulty breathing.

"What's going on?" Joe gasped. "What's happening?"

"Fire," Frank said. "We have to get out of here."

Together they put on their shoes, ran to the door of

their room, and undid the chain and the safety locks. Frank tried to open the door, but it wouldn't budge.

"It's stuck!" he cried.

Joe tried pulling on the door, but it still wouldn't open.

The smoke was now so thick in the room that the boys could barely see.

"We'll have to use the windows," Joe said.

The Hardy boys dropped to the floor to get under the smoke and started crawling toward the nearest window. Several times they got so disoriented by the smoke that they had to go back to their beds and start all over again.

Joe started to cough, and Frank was afraid that he was going to pass out. By the time they finally reached a window, though, Joe had stopped coughing.

Frank used the windowsill to pull himself up. He unlatched the window's lock—but when he tried to raise the window, it wouldn't budge. At first he thought it was just stuck—but then he noticed something that sent chills down his spine.

"Joe—somebody has nailed the window shut," Frank managed to say. He ran his fingers over the heads of the nails. They were at random places at the bottom of the window frame. "Someone deliberately did this. We'll have to smash our way out."

Joe had started to cough violently. Frank knew

that this time he might not be able to stop.

Frank steeled himself and stood up in the acrid smoke. He began feeling his way around the room. He needed a chair to heave through the window. It was their only way out.

Finally he found what he was looking for: the straight-back chair his father used when he was sitting at the writing desk.

Frank picked it up, stumbled once, stubbed his toe twice, and finally managed to make it to the window. He set the chair down, fell to the floor, gulped in some of the less smoky air, then stood up again.

"Cover your face, Joe!" Frank shouted. He heaved the chair at the window with all of his might.

The chair smashed through with such force that almost all of the glass was blasted out. Cool, fresh air rushed into the room. Frank felt along the floor for Joe, lifted him onto his shoulder, and set him on the window ledge.

Frank leaned out the window himself, gulped some of the air, and then followed Joe onto the ledge. For a few seconds he surveyed the scene below.

What he saw puzzled him. There was no one around. *Where are the fire trucks?* he wondered. *Wasn't the hotel on fire?*

Just barely within Frank's reach were the upper limbs of a large tree that shaded their room. They'd have to climb down this tree to escape.

Frank looked over at Joe and saw that his brother

seemed to be recovering. "Do you remember how to do this?" Frank asked.

Joe grinned. "Remember? I'm the one who taught you how to climb out our bedroom window at home using that old tree."

Frank smiled back. Joe was right. He was more agile than a monkey when it came to climbing trees.

"Then let's do it," Frank said.

He reached out, grabbed what looked like the strongest limb near him, and swung off the ledge. The limb bent more than he thought it would and sent him plunging a few feet. His heart nearly stopped. Fortunately the limb held, and Frank managed to grab an even stronger limb and climbed to a perch from where he could help Joe.

Joe grabbed the same limb that Frank had used, went through the same bungee-cord experience that his brother had, and pulled himself onto the limb next to Frank.

Joe looked around. "Where is everybody?" he said.

"I was wondering the same thing when we were on the ledge," Frank told him. "I don't think the whole hotel is on fire."

"You mean the fire was confined to only our room?" Joe said.

"Actually, I don't think it was a fire," Frank said. "There were no flames anywhere."

"You mean . . . ," Joe started to say.

Frank nodded. "Somebody put some sort of device in our room that would fill it with smoke. Remember that we couldn't get the door open? Somebody fixed it so we'd never get it open," he explained. "The window had been nailed shut. We weren't supposed to escape. We were supposed to die of smoke inhalation."

The Hardy boys climbed the rest of the way down the tree and found themselves in a small garden at the side of the hotel.

They made their way out a gate and onto a narrow service drive that led to the front of the New Stanley. It was only when they reached Kimathi Street that they realized they were still in their pajamas.

Just as they started to enter the lobby, a car pulled away from the curb.

Joe glanced in its direction as it passed under a streetlight. "Frank!" he cried. "Look at that car."

Frank turned, but the vehicle was quickly out of sight. "What about it?"

"Andrews was driving—and I think Dr. Douglas was sitting beside him!" Joe said.

"What?" Frank cried. Suddenly it all made sense. Dr. Douglas was no professor. He was the man Harry Andrews had said would be coming to Nairobi in two days. "So Dr. Douglas was the one who put that smoke device inside our room? He

131

probably fixed the door so it wouldn't open and nailed the windows shut."

"He knew we'd be gone for a while," Joe said, "because we told him. I can't believe it."

When they entered the hotel's lobby, they had to put up with some stares. They were so excited about what they had just learned, though, that it didn't matter to them.

One of the police officers ran up to them, scowling. "Where have you been?" he demanded. "You must stop doing this. We have other things . . ."

Frank raised a hand to stop him. "Listen," he said. He wasn't in the mood for a lecture. By now other police officers and some of the hotel staff had joined them. "It's not what you think."

Frank proceeded to tell them everything that had happened in the last several minutes. From time to time Joe added some details that Frank had left out.

A panicked manager pushed through the crowd to call the fire department. He wanted to make sure that the rest of the hotel, indeed, wasn't on fire. After calling he took several of the staff with him up to the Hardys' floor to survey the damage.

Joe could see that the police officers who had heard their story no longer looked angry. In fact, they seemed in awe of the boys.

"I think some of us owe you an apology," one of the officers said.

"Forget about that," Joe said. "Would you please contact Dr. Malindi and tell him to meet us here at the hotel?"

"Why?" the other police officer asked.

"We have to save a black rhino," Frank said. "The man who wants to kill it is here in Nairobi."

14 Death of the Black Rhino

Within fifteen minutes Dr. Malindi was in the lobby of the New Stanley Hotel.

Joe told him about seeing Harry Andrews and the man who called himself Dr. Douglas.

"We need to move at once," Dr. Malindi said. He looked at Frank and Joe. "I know you've been through quite an ordeal tonight. Are you sure you're up to this?"

The Hardy boys pronounced themselves ready for action.

"We want to catch these men as much as you do," Joe said. "The black rhino is not the only thing they're interested in killing."

A police car was waiting in front of the hotel.

Dr. Malindi got in the front seat with the driver, and Frank and Joe climbed into the back. The driver pulled out into Kimathi Street and headed toward the Hotel Zebra. Just as they turned onto River Road, the radio crackled, and a voice told Dr. Malindi that Room 37 in the hotel was vacant.

"Where could they have gone?" Dr. Malindi said.

The Hardy boys thought for a minute.

"I know someone who might know," Joe said. "The shopkeeper at Mombasa Curios."

The driver made a U-turn and drove back to Moi Avenue. There were no cars parked on the side of the street in front of Mombasa Curios, but the driver, at Dr. Malindi's request, parked several doors away.

"We don't want this car to alert them," Dr. Malindi said. "It is very important that we take them by surprise."

At this hour the shop was closed. The boys noticed lights in the windows above, which they thought might be where the shopkeeper and his wife lived.

Dr. Malindi suggested that the driver and Joe knock on the door and pretend to be frustrated tourists who had forgotten to buy some souvenirs and wouldn't have a chance tomorrow because of an early morning flight back to the United States.

Dr. Malindi and Frank would remain in the shadows, a few feet away, until the door was opened.

What if they don't open it? Frank thought.

After a few minutes a light went on in the shop, and someone started to unlatch the front door.

"We're closed," the shopkeeper's wife said. "What was it you wanted?"

The driver went into his act. His American accent would have fooled most people. The shopkeeper's wife let them know that letting tourists in was an imposition at this time of night. She told them they could come in, but she certainly hoped they made it worth her while.

When the shop door was fully opened, Dr. Malindi and Frank rushed out of the shadows and quickly followed the driver and Joe into the shop.

"What's the meaning of this?" the shopkeeper's wife demanded. "Who are you people?"

Dr. Malindi told her.

Now the woman was frightened. "No one is here. I don't know where they are. I have nothing to do with the hun—" Suddenly, she stopped, having realized that she had probably said too much already.

But one look from Dr. Malindi made her continue.

"They went to the Aberdares National Park," the woman said. "That's all I know. I won't say any more."

Dr. Malindi looked at Frank and Joe. "That's what we needed to know," he said. "That's one of the few places where black rhinos are left in Kenya."

They rushed out of the shop, leaving the woman staring after them.

"Do you think she'll contact them and tell them we're coming?" Joe asked as they ran toward the police car.

"This isn't America, Joe. Not everyone has a cell phone," Dr. Malindi said. "I doubt if anyone could reach them. They're probably in some old pickup truck that they borrowed from one of the locals. They'd be trying to look as unobtrusive as possible."

As they headed toward Wilson Airport to get a police helicopter to fly them north to the Aberdares National Park, Joe asked, "Why are there so few rhinos left?"

"Some foreigners think the rhino's horn has medicinal purposes," Dr. Malindi replied. "For one horn, they'll pay what most Kenyans would make in ten years of working at a regular job."

"I'm sure that's a big temptation for a lot of people," Frank said.

"It most certainly is," Dr. Malindi agreed. "The rhino population in Kenya in 1970 was twenty-two thousand. Today there are just a few hundred."

At Wilson Airport a member of Dr. Malindi's staff was waiting with the warm clothing and boots that the Hardy boys and Dr. Malindi would need for the Aberdares.

It took them only an hour by helicopter to reach the entrance to the park. They were met by Joshua Satima, one of the park officials. After introductions

137

Dr. Malindi and Frank and Joe got into Satima's Land Rover. They all headed into the park.

"Two men fitting the description you gave us were spotted in an old pickup at Tusk Hut, near Prince Charles Campsite," Satima told them. "Unfortunately our officers lost them in the darkness and the fog."

"Our luck," Dr. Malindi said.

"We're going to have our men stationed near the Ark and Treetops," Satima said. "That's where the black rhino are often seen in the early morning hours."

"There are only sixty black rhino in the park," Dr. Malindi added. "It's the largest indigenous population left in Kenya."

When they reached Tusk Hut, beyond Ruhuruini Gate, Satima turned right and headed toward Treetops.

Frank and Joe had heard about this famous "tree-hotel." Princess Elizabeth and Prince Philip were staying there when Elizabeth's father died and she became queen. From the rooms, which were built above watering holes, guests could watch all kinds of animals in their natural habitats.

When they reached Treetops, Satima said, "There's no road between here and the Ark. We have men watching the approaches to both tree-hotels, but we're going to walk a line between here and the Ark in hopes of surprising the poachers somewhere along the way. We think they'll follow the Thaara River—they're probably not all that familiar with the park, so they'll want to make sure they don't get lost."

Satima told everyone to keep conversation to a minimum. They wanted to make sure they could hear any animals—or humans—that were approaching.

Their trek took them through dense rain forest.

Two hours into the journey the sky above them began to show a lighter cast, signaling the approach of dawn.

An hour later they reached the Ark. They still hadn't seen either Andrews or the fake Dr. Douglas.

Satima had just suggested breakfast in the compound dining room when suddenly there was shouting on the north side of the compound.

Dr. Malindi, Mr. Satima, and the Hardy boys rushed north. They found some of the Ark staff trying to untie three uniformed park officials.

"This doesn't look good," Frank said to Dr. Malindi.

"I agree," Dr. Malindi said.

The three officials told a visibly angry Joshua Satima about how they'd been surprised by two men driving a dirty old pickup. It hadn't come from the south, as they had thought it would; it had come from the north, probably through the forest by way of Wanderis Gate.

"It never occurred to me that they'd come in that direction. It's out of the way," Satima said. "I thought they'd come in through Ruhuruini Gate."

"You were obviously wrong," Dr. Malindi said. Joe noticed the tension in the air. "Get on the radio, Satima, and have your men count the black rhinos."

Satima swallowed hard and did as Dr. Malindi asked. In the meantime Dr. Malindi took the Hardy boys to breakfast. Joshua Satima didn't accompany them. Just as they were finishing, Satima came into the dining room.

Dr. Malindi looked up. "Well?" he said, scarcely hiding the disdain in his voice.

"My men reported that there are fifty-nine rhinos, Dr. Malindi," Satima said.

"Fifty-nine," Dr. Malinda said. "Fifty-nine," he repeated after a minute. "That means one of them is missing. I'd venture a guess that it's in a dirty old pickup, headed for a secret slaughterhouse."

Joshua Satima hung his head.

Frank and Joe were devastated. They had been unable to save the black rhino.

When they finally got back to their hotel, Fenton Hardy was waiting for them in the lobby. He had been informed of their trip to the Aberdares National Park, but didn't know about the loss of the black rhino until Frank and Joe told him.

"I'm sorry, boys," he said. "You did everything you could to save it."

"I just want to go to bed," Joe said.

"Me, too," Frank agreed.

"Well, boys, I'm afraid that's out of the question. I got a telephone call early this morning. I'm needed on a case back in Bayport immediately," Mr. Hardy said. "I've already packed your suitcases. All of your clothes will need a good washing after being in all that smoke—I heard what happened. You boys never cease to amaze me with your bravery. Anyway, our flight leaves Nairobi in an hour."

With heavy hearts, the boys followed their father upstairs, picked up their suitcases, and headed toward the elevator.

"This is the first case we've ever lost," Joe said.

"I know," Frank said. "It's not a good feeling."

15 Watson's Surprise

Unlike the flight *to* Kenya, the flight back to John F. Kennedy International Airport was pretty uneventful. In fact, Frank and Joe slept most of the way.

The Hardy boys' van was out of the shop, so Callie Shaw and Iola Morton drove it to New York to pick up the Hardys.

"I'm looking forward to seeing Iola," Joe said as they headed toward the customs area. "We may go to a movie tonight."

"Do you want to double date?" Frank asked. "I was thinking about asking Callie if she wanted to go to one, too."

"Sure. Let's make a night out of it," Joe said. "We

can try that new Mexican restaurant in town."

The Hardys cleared customs without any trouble and made their way into the waiting area. Callie and Iola were there, jumping up and down and waving.

"It's so good to see you!" Callie told Frank. She gave him a big hug. "It seems like you've been gone for months!"

Iola hugged Joe and said, "More like years!"

"In a way," Frank said, "we've had the adventure of a lifetime."

Joe nodded.

As they all headed toward the parking garage, Frank and Joe started to fill the girls in on everything that had happened to them in Kenya.

When they reached the van, Mr. Hardy looked at his watch and said, "Let's make a detour, guys. We've got some time."

"Where to, Dad?" Frank asked. He was surprised at how much he wanted to get home to see the rest of their family and friends.

"Fifth Avenue Africana. I want to return Mr. Watson's books," Mr. Hardy replied. "They're rare. In fact, I didn't realize how rare they were until I had several people in Nairobi offer to pay me a fortune for them. I told the people to contact Mr. Watson, to see if he'd be interested in selling them. He needs to have them, in case he does decide to take the best offer."

Frank drove the van toward Manhattan. He decided to take I—495 to the Queens–Midtown Tunnel, which would put him just a few blocks south of Fifth Avenue Africana. They found a parking lot two blocks away from the shop.

"Let's all go. I want to thank Mr. Watson personally for the use of his books," Mr. Hardy said. "Then I think we should find an ice-cream shop. For the last few hours I've been thinking about nothing but milkshakes."

Everybody laughed.

They all walked the two blocks over to Fifth Avenue Africana. A sign on the door said that the shop would be closed for a few days.

"That's too bad," Mr. Hardy said. "We'll try to come down sometime next week."

"Wait, Dad! According to the dates on this sign, the shop is supposed to open again today," Joe said. "The first day it was closed was three days ago."

"Joe's right, Dad," Frank said. He suddenly had an idea. "Maybe Mr. Watson just got back and is working in his office." Frank started knocking heavily on the door. "I'm sure he won't mind getting his books back, especially if there are people who are willing to pay a lot of money for them."

After several hard knocks, which the Hardy boys were sure could have been heard in Mr. Watson's stockroom, there was still no answer. Mr. Hardy suggested that Frank and Joe return next week with the books.

Just then Iola said, "I think somebody's coming!"

The Hardy boys cupped their eyes with their hands and peered into the shop window.

"It's Mr. Watson," Joe said.

Mr. Watson looked out, smiled when he recognized the Hardys, and opened the door.

"Well, this is a pleasant surprise," he said.

"We just got back from Kenya," Joe said. "Dad wanted to return your books in person."

"Oh, well, that's very nice of you," Mr. Watson said. "I've always wanted to meet the famous Fenton Hardy." He held out his hands to receive the books. "I hope they helped."

"Yes, they did, very much," Mr. Hardy said. When Mr. Watson continued to remain where he was, Mr. Hardy added, "If it's not an imposition, I'd like to see your shop. The boys were impressed with your stock."

"Oh, of course. I'm sorry. I wasn't thinking," Mr. Watson said. He stepped away from the door to let them all come inside. "I just got back from a long trip myself, and I was trying to get some paperwork taken care of before I actually opened the shop for business."

"Well, we appreciate your accommodating us," Fenton Hardy said.

145

"Oh, I love this stuff!" Callie cried, browsing through the shelves.

"Me, too," Iola agreed. "It's so different from what we see in the stores in our mall."

Mr. Hardy told Mr. Watson about the offers he had had for the books that Mr. Watson had lent him. "I wanted to return them, in case some of the officials in Nairobi actually called you."

"Well, that's very kind of you," Mr. Watson said.

"Would you mind if my sons and I saw the rest of your book collection?" Mr. Hardy asked. "I'm thinking about starting my own."

"Oh, well, no, I wouldn't mind," Mr. Watson said. "I keep the rarest books in my office. It's this way."

While Callie and Iola looked around the shop, Mr. Hardy and the boys followed Mr. Watson to his office.

Mr. Watson opened the door and turned on the light. They all went inside.

Suddenly Joe stopped in his tracks. He looked at Frank and nodded toward an old-fashioned coatrack in the corner of the room. There were three things hanging on it: a sweat-stained pith helmet, a safari jacket, and a wooden cane with a carved baboon head.

The Hardy boys looked at each other and nodded. They knew what they had to do.

"Uh, Dr. Douglas, how is your research in Swahili dialects going?" Joe said.

Watson whirled around, a look of total surprise on his face. "How did you . . ." He stopped and looked at the coatrack in the corner. He turned to Mr. Hardy. "I can explain that," he stammered.

"Can you explain the death of the black rhino?" Frank demanded. "What have you done with the parts?"

"What are you talking about?" Watson demanded. "We didn't kill the black rhino. There were too many park police in the area. Somebody must have tipped them off."

For some reason Frank and Joe believed what Watson was saying—but they had to know for sure.

"Do you have Dr. Malindi's telephone number, Dad?" Frank asked. "I want to call him. There's something I need to ask."

Mr. Hardy withdrew Dr. Malindi's card from his wallet and handed it to Frank. Frank calculated the time difference between New York and Nairobi. "It's not too late," he said. "He should still be up."

Fenton Hardy handed Frank his cell phone, since it was enabled to make international calls.

Dr. Malindi answered on the third ring. Frank identified himself and then said that he had some good news—but that he needed to ask Dr. Malindi a question first.

"By any chance have the authorities recounted the black rhino herd in the Aberdares National Park?" Frank said.

He listened for several minutes, smiled, then said, "Good. That's what I was hoping to hear. Oh, by the way, we've caught 'Dr. Douglas.' Yes, that's right. I'm sure the police here will be in touch with you." Frank listened for a couple of minutes, then ended the conversation with, "We appreciate all you did for us, too."

"Well," Joe said. "Let's hear it."

"There are still sixty black rhino in the Aberdares National Park," Frank reported. "The missing one was found several hours later, after we had already left Kenya, hiding in some thick undergrowth."

"They're obviously smarter than most people give them credit for," Joe said. "That rhino probably knew what was in store for him if he didn't do something like that."

"See! Andrews and I didn't do anything wrong," Watson said. "Now, I think you need to leave my shop."

"Not so fast, Watson," Fenton Hardy said.

"I guess you've forgotten about murder and attempted murder," Frank said. "It's because of you and Harry Andrews that somebody pulled the life-support plugs on our friend Robert Namanga at the hospital in Nairobi."

"And Frank and I could have died from smoke inhalation in the New Stanley Hotel, too. That was your doing," Joe added. "Dr. Malindi said that the police have already closed down Mombasa Curios and have taken the shopkeeper and his wife into custody, and now they want to talk to you and Andrews. They're going to have you extradited to Kenya after the New York police have finished with their investigation."

Watson paled. "What investigation?"

"I'm sure that if the police looked around this shop, they'd find some illegal animal parts," Frank said.

Joe dialed a number on his cell phone. "And there's no telling what they'll find when they visit Harry Andrews at his house in Long Island City, either," he added.

"Who are you calling?" Watson demanded.

"A friend of mine in the New York City Police Department," Joe replied. "Officer Al Fielding."

"Al Fielding!" Fenton Hardy exclaimed.

"Not the Al Fielding you worked with, Dad. It's his son," Frank explained. "We forgot to tell you that we ran into him the other day."

Fenton Hardy raised an eyebrow. "You did?"

Frank nodded. "We'll tell you all about it on the way back to Bayport."

While Mr. Hardy kept watch over Watson until

the police arrived, Frank and Joe went into the shop to see how Callie and Iola were doing.

"Oh, Frank!" Callie said. "These carved animals are beautiful!"

"Callie and I have made a decision, Joe. We're all going to Africa together on a safari next year!" Iola said. "That way, we can see all of the *real* wild animals—and even sleep out under the stars."

Frank and Joe groaned.

"Sorry, Iola. The closest I'm getting to Africa anytime soon is at the movies," Joe said, and yawned. "In fact, there's a new one set in Kenya that opens tonight. I saw it advertised on a billboard near the airport. I'll take you to that."

Iola sighed. "Well, okay. It's not exactly the same thing," she said, "but I guess it's better than nothing."

Callie looked at Frank. "What about us?"

"You want to go, too?" Frank said. He let out a big yawn. "Joe and I are both still on Kenya time. If we're together, we can keep each other awake. I don't want to suffer any more jet lag than I need to."

"Oooh, this is going to be a *really* exciting date," Iola said, smirking. "I can already tell!"

"I have a better idea," Callie said. "Iola, why don't we go to the movie by ourselves and *pretend* the guys are there?"

"Okay, okay, we get it," Frank said. "We promise to stay awake!"

"Sounds good. And who knows?" Iola nudged Joe in the arm. "If you keep your eyes open, you might find another mystery to solve on the way to the theater."

Frank and Joe looked at each other and smiled. That was a definite possibility.

The most puzzling mysteries . . .
The cleverest crimes . . .
The most dynamic brother detectives!

THE HARDY BOYS®

FRANKLIN W. DIXON

Join Frank and Joe Hardy in up-to-date
adventures packed with action and suspense

Look for brand-new mysteries
wherever books are sold.

Available from Aladdin Paperbacks
Published by Simon & Schuster